THE MASKED MARKSMAN:
DEATH'S UNDERSTUDY
AND OTHER STORIES

DEATH'S UNDERSTUDY
AND OTHER STORIES

By Emile C. Tepperman

POPULAR PUBLICATIONS • 2024

PUBLISHING HISTORY

"Juggler's Holiday" originally appeared in the July, 1935 (Vol. 6, No. 2) issue of *The Spider* magazine. "Death's Curtain-Call" originally appeared in the August, 1935 (Vol. 6, No. 3) issue of *The Spider* magazine. "Cue for a Gunman" originally appeared in the October, 1935 (Vol. 7, No. 1) issue of *The Spider* magazine. "Murder Backstage" originally appeared in the November, 1935 (Vol. 7, No. 2) issue of *The Spider* magazine. "Death's Understudy" originally appeared in the December, 1935 (Vol. 7, No. 3) issue of *The Spider* magazine. "Action Off Stage" originally appeared in the January, 1936 (Vol. 7, No. 4) issue of *The Spider* magazine. "Prologue to Death" originally appeared in the February, 1936 (Vol. 8, No. 1) issue of *The Spider* magazine. Copyright 2024 by Argosy Communications, Inc. All rights reserved.

Visit POPULARPUBLICATIONS.com for more books like this.

JUGGLER'S HOLIDAY

E D RACE was due at the Clyde Theater ten minutes after ten for his gun-juggling number. He was shaving in the bathroom of his single room at the Longmont Hotel when the insistent rapping came at the door.

He had just stepped out of the shower, letting the water drip from him while he shaved. The left side of his face, as well as his chin, was still lathered.

He grumbled impatiently and went to the door still dripping, still clutching the razor. He was thinking grouchily that the tailor always managed to bring his suits back at the most inconsiderate times.

He yanked the door open savagely, saying, "Why the hell can't you—"

Then he stopped short, gulping. "Hey! You can't come in here! Say—"

The girl evidently didn't even hear him. She had been looking behind her, with a frightened face; but now she sprang inside, breathing hard.

Ed closed the door, dropped the razor, and reached back to the bed. He dragged off the top sheet and covered himself hastily with it.

"My God, Miss Partages! Why don't you look where you leap!"

He knew her. Elsie Partages, daughter of fat, generous Leon Partages, who owned the string of theaters of which the Clyde was the largest. Elsie's father was the man who paid Ed's salary.

Ed Race, THE MASKED MARKSMAN of vaudeville fame. His gun-juggling and shooting act was headlined all over the country, and he had no rivals. He was billed as "The Man Who Could Make Guns Talk." And he did just that. Not satisfied with his stage success, however, he had turned his attention to another field in his insatiable search for excitement. The investigation of crime—pursued as a sort of sideline. He had licenses which permitted him to operate as a private detective in a dozen states.

Few people knew Ed Race was THE MASKED MARKSMAN; fewer still knew he was interested in detective work. But those few had taken advantage of such knowledge to call upon him whenever they got in a jam.

He shrugged resignedly as he gazed into the white, frightened face of Elsie Partages. She was in trouble apparently—and had naturally come to him.

Her eyes were like those of some hunted thing. She wore no hat, and her dress was rumpled and torn at the right shoulder. Her breast was heaving spasmodically. Her gaze darted around the room to the open window. Swiftly she ran across, closed it, set the catch, and pulled down the shade.

"Mr. Race!" she exclaimed. "Help me, please. Don't let them get me!"

"Don't let *who* get you?"

"Those men. There were three of them. They killed Roy Santis,

upstairs in Room 640. They shot him until he was dead, with long guns that had funny things on the ends and didn't make any noise at all."

She came up to him eagerly. "You must do something, Mr. Race. Roy's dead up there, and I was seen to go up with him. The police will be looking for me. If dad ever found out—" She caught her breath, added almost inaudibly: "I was such a fool, I—I was—going to elope with Roy!"

"What? *You* elope with Roy Santis! The guy that's almost been classed as Public Enemy Number One—except that the cops couldn't ever get anything on him!"

SHE LOWERED her eyes. "I—I didn't know it—not till one

3

of those men who shot him told me. It seems he double-crossed them, or something. Here—" She reached into the blouse of her dress, drew forth a stone strangely iridescent in the half-light of the room.

Ed had seen valuable stones before. He whistled. "Boy! That must be worth—"

"A hundred and fifty thousand. It's the Cawnpore Pearl. Roy Santis and those three men held up the messenger from Bellamy's last week—you saw it in the paper, I suppose?"

Ed held out his hand, and she dropped the glowing gem into his palm. He turned it over in his fingers. Then he frowned as he noted two small scratches at one point on the surface. They were not imperfections, and he wondered how they had got there.

He shrugged. There were more important things to consider at the moment.

He looked up at the girl. "How did you get this?"

"Roy gave it to me. He said it was a wedding present. He told me to hide it until we were married and out of the country. I didn't know it was the Cawnpore Pearl. Then when those men broke in, they wanted to know where it was; they searched the room. I got scared and ran out—they weren't paying me much attention, because they thought I'd fainted."

Ed considered. And then he said: "You wait here till I get the rest of this beard off my face. Then I'll take you downtown and see if I can get Inspector Hansen to put the hush-hush on your part in it."

Ed picked up his razor and went into the bathroom, taking the pearl along with him. He closed the door, thrust the sheet into a corner, and started to lather his face all over again. He scowled at his reflection in the mirror.

The girl who was waiting for him out there in the next room had always been a problem to her father. Her mother had died ten years ago, and she had grown up willful, spoiled. She was not inherently bad, but she seemed to have a faculty for doing things that got in the newspapers and embarrassed her father. Like this business of eloping with Santis.

HE HAD almost finished shaving when someone knocked heavily at the outer door. He heard Elsie Partages ask in a shaky voice: "W-who's there?"

"Damn that girl!" he growled to himself. "Why couldn't she keep still!"

From outside someone exclaimed triumphantly: "She's in here, Mac. I told you she'd go lookin' for Race!"

Ed was beginning to get tired of this. He put the razor down with a sigh, wound the bath towel around his middle, and tied it in a knot at the side. He opened the bathroom door. The girl was standing rooted to the floor.

At the same instant two shots—muffled, in quick succession—tore into the lock, and the door swung free. Those chaps outside were men of action, all right.

Ed's guns were with his clothes on the bed across the room, near the door. It was too late to get them. A big broad-faced man had appeared in the doorway. He held a silenced automatic in his big ham of a fist, and his face did not reflect the slightest excitement. Behind him were two others, attired like the first in tan topcoats and tan slouch hats, each with a silenced gun.

5

The big man looked from the girl to Ed and started to grin. "Just a little party, hey? Suppose you hold it like that!"

Instead, Ed swept up a heavy ashtray from the end table close to his left hand and with a single continuous motion hurled it at the face of the man in the doorway. And then he gasped out a wild curse, for Elsie Partages had chosen just that second to recover from her fright and take a single involuntary step forward, which brought her in line with the missile. It struck her a glancing blow across the forehead, and she stumbled, gasped, and fell forward into the big man's arms.

The other two had shoved into the room, however, and now their guns menaced Ed. So he did the only thing he could have done under the circumstances: He ducked back into the bathroom, slammed the door, and sidestepped just as a hail of lead smashed through the thin wood.

Suddenly the shooting ceased. The same voice he had heard before ordered, "Get in there and take him, Mac. He ain't got a gun!"

Ed leaned over and catch-locked the door. He grinned as the knob was turned.

"Hello, Sid. He's locked himself in!"

"All right. Shoot the lock out!"

Ed didn't wait. He snatched up the Cawnpore Pearl, which he had left beside the shaving cream and, giving a last yank to the knot that held the towel about him, he scrambled up on the washbasin and pushed open the window. He was outside, clinging to the sill, when the first of several shots shattered the lock.

He put the pearl in his mouth, reached up with one hand and

closed the window. The sill to which he clung was in reality a long ledge extending across the wall of the hotel.

AS HE worked along the ledge he expected any moment to hear the shouts of someone from the building opposite. But no alarm was raised. He heard the bathroom window opening and knew that in another moment he would be a splendid target. It was a good time to get off the ledge, and he did. He had traveled about six feet, and was at an open window. This would be the room next to his. He didn't know who occupied it, but there was no time to be squeamish. So he heaved himself up and vaulted in.

The bright sunlight had partly blinded him, and he didn't know anybody was in there until a masculine voice said hoarsely, "Hey, you! What you doing there?"

He couldn't answer because he had the pearl in his mouth. He raised his hand to take it out, and the voice snapped, "Don't move! I've got you covered!"

Ed stood still. Slowly his eyes got accustomed to the semi-gloom, and he saw a small, bald-headed man sitting on the bed holding a revolver shakily and—even then—reaching for the telephone.

He spat out the pearl, which rolled along the carpet. "Wait, mister. I can explain all this. There's some men in my room—"

The little man grunted. "You can tell it to the police." He scanned Ed's appearance. "Imagine it! Breaking in here through the window, half naked—hello, hello. Operator! Send up the house detective at once, and notify the police. I've caught a burglar in my room, a *naked* burglar! Yes, that's what I said—a naked burglar! If you don't believe me come up and see for yourself!"

He hung up with a bang, and glared over the sights of his revolver. "Back home we hear a lot about the New York bandits, but I swear—we never read about no robbers goin' around dressed in bath towels! I bet my name will be in the papers on account of this. Maybe even my picture!"

Ed stood there resignedly. He didn't make any sudden moves. If the little man got scared, the revolver might go off. Ed knew how to handle men who were accustomed to guns; but he had learned that a person like this could be more dangerous than a real killer.

It seemed like an hour before someone rapped at the door.

The little man called out, "All right, Mister Detective—just a minute." And then: "You, Mister Burglar, just go over there and open that door." Ed obeyed as quickly as possible.

Halloran, the house detective, was a big, husky, redheaded chap, and when he saw Ed in the towel he burst out laughing. The little man got off the bed and asked testily: "What you laughing at? Think this is a joke? This here burglar climbed in through the window. If Emma hadn't of made me bring along my revolver, he'd of killed me. O' course, I was so excited I clean forgot it wasn't loaded!"

ED STARTED to swear, and Halloran burst out laughing more loudly than ever.

"This is rich, Race. Imagine Ed Race being bagged by a guy from the sticks, with a gun that wasn't loaded!" He clapped Ed on the back. "Wait'll I tell this story around!"

Ed rubbed his bare shoulder where the other had slapped him.

"You win, Halloran. The joke's on me. Now let's get serious. There's a girl in my room, and three gunmen that are after her."

"No!" Halloran exclaimed. He got out his own revolver and said to the little man, "Give Mr. Race that gun of yours, will you?"

The little man protested incredulously. "What! Give a burglar my gun? Not—"

Halloran snatched the gun out of his hand and handed it to Ed. "He's not a burglar, Mister, he's an actor—which is almost as bad. Come on, Race, let's go!"

But Ed was already out of the room and in the corridor before his own door. The door was partly open, with the lock sagging out where it had been shot away.

As Halloran joined him, with the little man peering out from his own doorway, Ed kicked the door wide and stepped inside.

The room was empty.

Halloran came in and stood beside him. He was grinning again. "Sure you wasn't dreaming this thing, Race? Sounds kind of phony to me. Three guys gunning for a girl, an' you in the next room with a towel."

Ed stirred impatiently. "Don't be a dope, Halloran. Those guys were here. They must have gone down while you were coming up. I wonder how they got her out of here—"

"Hey!" Halloran almost shouted. "Wait a minute. I saw them!"

"Where!"

"They were coming out of the elevator just as I got in—three guys in tan coats, and this girl in a blue dress and no hat. I thought they looked kind of funny. Two of these guys were close to the girl on either side of her and they had their hands in their pockets. She walked kind of wobbly, but I was in a hurry to get up here and didn't pay them much attention."

"They were the ones," Ed said grimly. "They've got away."

He turned to see the little man standing in the doorway, holding something in his hand. It was the Cawnpore Pearl.

"I found this on the floor," he said.

"Is it—"

Ed snatched it from him. "It is. I spit it there."

"You *what?*"

Ed pushed him out of the room. "I'll write you a letter about it sometime," he said. "Right now I'm busy." He closed the door.

The little man called through testily, "This is a damn nuisance. I'm going to check out of here!" Ed paid him no attention, just started scrambling into his clothes, not bothering even to shave his upper lip.

Halloran watched him, puzzled. "This is a hell of a note," he complained. "You go running around the hotel naked, you have dames and gunmen coming up here, and now a guest is going to check out. Where do you get this stuff?"

Ed stooped over to lace his shoes. "If it'll make you feel any better," he said cheerfully, "I'll tell you there's a stiff in Room 640, too. Laugh that off!"

Halloran almost burned his fingers on the cigar he was lighting. "A stiff! My Gawd. Who?"

"Roy Santis. This pearl is part of the swag from the Bellamy job. The guys that were in here are the ones that knocked off Santis. Two of 'em are called Sid and Mac. I didn't get the name of the other guy. Santis was going to double-cross them and lam with the jewel, taking the girl along. So they bopped him. The girl had the pearl, and she got away and ran down here, for me."

HALLORAN TRIED another match with a hand that shook a little. "Geez," he exclaimed, "this is terrible. Roy Santis knocked off in this dump? I never even knew he was staying here. The boss will can me for this." He sighed. "Who was the girl?"

"I don't know. She just ran in on me."

Halloran squinted at him through a cloud of cigar smoke. "Nerts. You trying to tell me it was just coincidence, her picking your room?"

"Take it or leave it," Ed told him shortly. He finished lacing his shoes and hastily examined the two revolvers in his shoulder holsters. They were two of the heavy forty-fives he used in his act. He preferred them to lighter guns because he was used to the heft of them.

He had already started for the door when the 'phone rang.

He answered it, and started slightly when he heard the voice of Leon Partages on the other end, talking at a mile-a-minute rate.

The theater owner was beside himself with anxiety. "Look here, Ed, this is terrible. I just got a 'phone call from some man, and he says he's got Elsie a prisoner and he'll kill her if you don't do what he says."

"What does he say?" Ed demanded, trying to make his tone casual for the benefit of Halloran.

"He says Elsie had a pearl or something and she gave it to you. She told him she did. Well, he wants you to turn the pearl over to him, or else he'll kill Elsie." Partages' voice cracked slightly. "Ed, what's this terrible thing all about? Has he really got Elsie?"

Ed gulped. How could he tell this doting father that his only daughter had been about to elope with Roy Santis, that she was actually involved in this sordid business?

He said into the mouthpiece, "It's all right. There's nothing to worry about. Did the man say how or where I was to return the—" He stopped, saw that Halloran was listening, and finished: "—the—thing?"

"You mean the pearl? Yes. He said you should take a cab from the Longmont and drive south on Broadway, slowly, until a man got in with you. You're to give the man the pearl, and they'll release Elsie in a half-hour."

"Okay," Ed said. "I'll do that. Don't worry, everything is jake."

He hung up and said, "I've got to go now, Halloran. See you later."

But the detective barred his way. "Wait a minute, Race." He looked at Ed very queerly. "What's this stuff you're pulling? You going to leave me holding the bag, with a stiff in Room 640 and a guest next door checking out? Nix. Lemme turn in the pearl at least, so I can square things with the cops. They'll overlook a lot if I give 'em a chance to take credit for recovering the Bellamy swag."

Ed turned cold. He'd forgotten that he had told Halloran

about the Cawnpore Pearl. He couldn't have avoided it anyway because Halloran had seen the little man give it to him.

He shrugged. Partages deserved a break.

"Look, Halloran," he said earnestly. "Suppose you forget about that pearl. There's a girl's life in the balance, and I've got to give the stone back to save her. Make believe you didn't see it. I think I can get you a handsome present—say a couple of centuries."

Halloran shook his head. "Nix, Race. That's got to be reported to the police. Don't forget, the guy next door knows about it, and he'll blab his head off to the cops."

Halloran stopped suddenly, and his eyes narrowed. "Sa-ay! What's this, anyway? You seem to know an awful lot about the whole thing, for having got into it accidental like. How do I know you wasn't in with Santis and that crowd? I think I'll call up headquarters right now. I ain't getting the hotel in dutch any more than I can help."

He started for the 'phone. "You wait right here, Race, while I call up. Inspector Hansen will want to talk to you."

Ed sighed. "I hate to do this, Halloran," he said softly, "but I got to get that girl out of a jam."

Halloran stopped short, half turned, and said, "Do what?"

"This!"

Ed's bunched fist flashed up in a short swing that landed with a thud behind the big detective's right ear.

Halloran grunted and sank to the floor.

Ed worked swiftly. He took off Halloran's tie, gagged him with it, strapped his wrists behind his back with his belt, dragged him over to the bed, and laid him there. Halloran was breathing regularly. He'd have little difficulty freeing himself when he came to.

ED HURRIED out to the elevators then. He found himself still holding the empty revolver Halloran had taken from the little man next door, and he thrust it into his coat pocket.

The door of number 512, the little man's room, was closed. He considered going in and returning the revolver, but there was no time for that. He pressed the button for the elevator, descended to the lobby, and crossed to the clerk's desk. The Longmont was a small hotel, and the clerk operated the switchboard himself.

He wore a worried frown as Ed approached. "What's up, Mr. Race? Mr. Smallwood in Room 512 'phoned down—"

"He had a bad dream," Ed interrupted. "There's nothing to it. Did you 'phone headquarters?"

"Certainly, sir. A radio car should be—"

"When they get here, tell them to go up to Room 640. Don't tell them anything about that little runt in 512. He's had enough trouble with his bad dreams already. He says he's going to check out."

The clerk smiled. "It doesn't matter, Mr. Race. He intended to check out anyway." He showed Ed a long railroad ticket. "He asked us yesterday to get him a ticket for Chicago. He's leaving on the one o'clock train."

"Give him this," Ed said, laying the revolver on the desk. "And tell him it's a good thing for him it wasn't loaded. I bet he doesn't even know you need a license to carry one in this town!"

Hurrying out, Ed hailed a cab. As he was getting in he saw a radio car pull up to the curb. He grinned. The clerk would send the cops up to 640, and when they found the body of Santis they'd be too busy to go looking for Halloran.

"Where to, mister?" the cabby inquired.

"Go slow down Broadway," Ed told him. "I'm picking up a friend along here somewhere."

He sat well forward so that he could be seen from the street. "Slower," he directed in a moment.

They traveled at a snail's pace for almost three blocks, and Ed began to think something had slipped.

Then the cab was halted for a red light, and someone opened the door quickly and got in beside him. It was Sid—the big man at whom he had thrown the ashtray.

Ed said, "Where's the girl?"

The man grunted and put out his hand. "Where's the pearl?" His other hand was in his jacket pocket, and the outline of the silencer on the muzzle of his gun was visible through the cloth.

Ed's eyes locked with his. "No girl, no pearl," he said.

The man snarled. "You crossin' us, Race?"

"No." Ed's voice was calm. "I just want to make sure you don't cross me. I'm taking a big chance, as it is. The cops are sure to find out I turned the pearl back to you, and then I'm going to be in one hell of a jam. I don't want to do that for nothing. When I see the girl I'll give you the sparkler."

Sid seemed to think that over, studying Ed all the time. Finally he shrugged. "All right. You got the pearl with you?"

Ed nodded.

"Let's see it."

15

"Nix. When I see Elsie Partages."

"Okay, Race. But if you're crossin' us—"

"I'm not. Where do we go?"

Sid tapped on the glass. "Drive west, to the river," he instructed the cabby.

It took sixteen minutes to cover the five blocks to the riverfront, with lights at each corner. Neither Ed nor the big man said another word. But they watched each other carefully. The big man never took his hand from his pocket.

AT TWELFTH AVENUE they got out and Ed paid off the driver. They watched the cab disappear up the street, and then Sid said curtly, "This way. You try any tricks an' the girl is as good as croaked."

"I won't try any tricks," Ed told him. "I only want to get her away."

Sid nodded, starting south, walking warily alongside.

"Just to keep the record clear," Ed said, "I'd like to warn you not to try any tricks yourself. Ever hear of THE MASKED MARKSMAN?"

"Sure. Seen him in vaudeville. Don't tell me you're him!"

Ed's hand flashed to his armpit, and in a motion so fast the other was unaware he had begun it, he had his heavy revolver out and was poking it into Sid's side.

The big man turned white, gulped. His own hand was frozen inside his pocket, on the butt of the silenced gun. He was caught flat.

Ed grinned, holstered the revolver again. "That was just to warn you not to try anything. There's three of you where we're going. I'm going to give you the pearl, and you're going to let me walk out with the girl. Otherwise it'll be too bad for a couple of you. Clear?"

"Hell," said the big man. "We won't stop you."

They turned at the next corner and Sid led the way down an alley, then through a side door into a low, one-story building that had at some time in the past been a junk shop of some sort but was not untenanted.

The office was in the rear, and here they found the other two men who had broken into Ed's room.

In a corner, on a chair, sat Elsie Partages. She was not tied but sat quite still, evidently in fear of her guards. But she jumped up when she saw Ed, ran to him, threw her arms around his neck and started to sob. Ed pushed her off roughly. He wanted elbow room.

Sid explained to the other two that Ed had the pearl with him. The tall, thin one said, "All right, guy. Let's see it."

Ed stepped back to the wall, drew the pearl from his vest pocket, and flipped it across. The thin man's eyes lighted as he caught it dexterously.

Elsie exclaimed, "Ed! Are you going to take me out of here?" She gripped his right arm, and once more he had to shake her off. He tensed.

He was watching Sid, who had taken the pearl now and was examining it closely. He looked up suddenly and snarled. "You're crossin' us, Race. This ain't the Cawnpore Pearl!"

Ed looked unbelieving. "So that's the stunt, is it? You're not crossing me at all, are you?" He grew ugly. "Listen, you—that's the stone this girl gave me. She got it from Santis. And if it isn't the Cawnpore Pearl, then Santis put one over on her and on you, too!"

Sid shook his head. "Santis didn't put anything over. This here is a perfect imitation of the Cawnpore Pearl, an' he wouldn't of had a chance in the world to have such an imitation made. We shadowed him every minute of the time."

ED GLANCED from one to another of them. The other two were just waiting for a word from Sid.

"How do you know that's a phony?"

The big man answered heavily, "We found out how Bellamy's marked it. They had a secret mark on it, because there was word going around that a certain slick confidence man was coming to town to work a substitution gag on them, with a perfect imitation. So they had two little dots cut into the real stone, and the clerks in the store were supposed to look for them every time they handled the pearl." Sid held the stone up under the electric light. "Well, there ain't any marks on this one. This is phony."

Ed's body was taut. He saw in their eyes the conviction that they had been hoaxed; saw their determination to kill.

Alone, he would have shot it out with them, willingly matching his skill and speed against their numbers. But with Elsie Partages beside him, it was a different matter. If the fireworks started, he couldn't possibly prevent her death.

"Listen," he said desperately. "This girl knows nothing about the pearl. She just took what Santis gave her and kept it for him. You don't think she got this phony and switched it on you—"

"No," said the thin man, who stood at his right. "But we think maybe *you* did. You got one chance, Race. Do you come across, or do we start shooting?"

Ed's eyes narrowed. His arms were crooked at the elbows, ready to flash in and out of his armpit holsters. Death faced them both here—him and the girl. These men couldn't be talked out of it.

Suddenly they all stiffened, froze.

From the doorway came a sharp, incisive voice.

"Don't move. You're all covered!"

In the doorway stood Detective Sergeant Steve Bland, whom Ed knew well. Behind him, in the gloom of the junk shop, were Halloran and Smallwood, the little man who had threatened to check out of the Longmont.

Ed stepped away from the wall, pushed Elsie Partages behind him. "Stay back, kid," he whispered. "There's going to be fireworks."

There was. Sid and the other two weren't going to be taken.

Sergeant Bland was just saying: "Race, where do you get that stuff, tying Halloran up? It's a good thing I thought of going to your room. And found the cab driver who brought you here. He thought it was a phony set-up, and he watched where you went—"

Sid cried hoarsely, "Let's take 'em!"

They fired from their pockets.

Steve Brand staggered, as the small office rocked to the explosions of his own .38. He stumbled backward into Halloran, still firing into the room.

The echoes of the .38 were almost drowned by the deeper roar of Ed's two .45s. He had flashed them out almost as the firing began, had shot three times.

When the smoke cleared away, Bland wobbled into the room, supported by Halloran, while Smallwood danced in after them.

The sergeant glanced down at the three bodies on the floor, looked over at Ed, who was holding Elsie Partages in his arms. She had fainted.

"Hell," said Sergeant Bland, "you never leave anybody alive. I can't chalk up arrests with corpses!"

Ed said sourly over his shoulder, "When guys with guns are blasting at you, Steve, it's always safest to shoot to kill. You hurt bad?"

"No. It's a flesh wound." Bland stooped and picked up from the floor, where Sid had dropped it, the glowing pearl. "Ye Gods!" he exclaimed. "This is the Cawnpore Pearl!"

Elsie had opened her eyes, and Ed sat her in a chair. "Keep your eyes closed, kid," he told her. "I'll take you out in a couple of minutes."

Then he swung to Bland. "That's—not the Cawnpore Pearl, Steve," he said. "It's a phony. Somebody switched it."

Bland examined it closely. "You're right. There's supposed to be a couple of secret marks—"

HALLORAN LOOKED appealingly at Ed.

"*Geez*, Race, didn't these guys have the real stone, after all? Can't—"

"Wait a minute," Ed broke in. He buttonholed Bland. "Look, Steve, I'll make a bargain with you. Elsie Partages, here, didn't have anything to do with the Bellamy job. She witnessed the murder of Santis, but the three guys who did it are dead; so you don't need her for anything. If I turn up the real Cawnpore Pearl, will you give her a break, and see to it that she's not mentioned at all?"

Bland grumbled: "Okay. You turn it up, I'll keep her out of it, and we split the reward three ways—you, me, and Halloran. Too bad I can't make a pinch, so as to get credit for an arrest, too."

"I'll give you a pinch, too, Steve," Ed told him softly.

Halloran was staring at him open-mouthed. Bland asked unbelievingly: "What you going to do—pull it out of your hat?"

"No," said Ed. "There's your pinch!"

He swung and pointed at the mousy looking Smallwood, who had been edging toward the door. "That's your confidence man who came to New York to try to ring in a phony instead of the Cawnpore Pearl. Only he was too late, because Santis and these other muggs beat him to it by pulling the robbery. He had the imitation with him, and when he found the real one on the floor, he just switched them, and returned the phony to me!"

Halloran exclaimed: "Well, I'll be a monkey's uncle! Small—"

Mr. Smallwood was no longer a mousy sort of person. He sprang backward, got behind Elsie Partages' chair and seized her from behind, around the throat. His free hand produced a small automatic, as if by magic.

"Stand back, you dicks!" he snarled. "Or I'll let the girl have it! She's walking out of here with me, and you're going to like it. Drop your guns, quick—"

His last words were drowned by the terrific thunder of Ed's .45.

21

Smallwood had been stooping behind Elsie's chair, so that only the top of his head had been visible. But Ed's slug found its mark in his forehead, and he was hurled backward as if he had been kicked. His grip was torn from Elsie's throat, and the automatic exploded once in the air, spinning out of his lifeless hand.

When the reverberations died away, Bland exclaimed: "God, that was close shooting, Race! I wouldn't've had the guts to try it. A half-inch lower, and you'd have killed Miss Partages!"

Ed was already stooping beside Smallwood's body, going through his pockets. "Hell," he said, "I couldn't miss. Don't I practice enough?"

His fingers came out of Smallwood's vest pocket with a stone that shone a gorgeous deep purple under the electric light. The imitation, which Bland still held, was pale, lifeless, by comparison.

"That's the goods!" Halloran said. "Boy, what a beauty!"

Ed handed the stone to Bland. "There you are, Steve." He went over to Elsie Partages, patted her on the back. "It's all over now, kid. You can go back to your old man and tell him to give you a good licking."

"What I don't understand," Halloran was musing, "is how the devil Race got wise to this here Smallwood. He looked so innocent and helpless—"

Ed turned away from Elsie, grinning. "Just a small mistake he made, Halloran. He said he was checking out because he was annoyed, and all the time he had intended to leave at one o'clock today. And he laid it on a little too thick about the folks back home, and getting his picture in the paper."

Sergeant Bland winced, touched his wounded arm. "I never suspected him. I just dragged him along with us, because Halloran was sore at you and wanted Smallwood to sign a complaint against you. He didn't want to come, but I made him."

"All right," Halloran said sheepishly, "I *was* sore. So would anybody be when he gets socked behind the ear. What I want to know, though, is what made you so sure, Race, that Smallwood had the pearl. Just his talking—"

Ed was ejecting the spent shells from his revolvers, replacing them with fresh cartridges. "It wasn't just his talking, Halloran. There was one thing more. I'd noticed those scratches on the pearl myself, when Elsie gave it to me. And the only time it was out of my sight after that was when I dropped it in Smallwood's room. So he was the only one who *could* have switched them!"

Sergeant Bland sighed, dropped the stones in his pocket. His left arm was hanging limp at his side. "Let's get out of here," he said, "so I can have my wing fixed up." He glared at Ed. "And next time, I wish you'd leave somebody alive so I can make a pinch!"

DEATH'S CURTAIN-CALL

THE FAÇADE of the three-story brownstone building bore nothing to indicate the nature of its occupancy except for a small, metal plaque alongside the door, above the bell. The bronze letters on the plaque read:

THE THIRTEEN CLUB

Ed Race strode past the building with an air of casualness, but his quick glance took in the heavy, oak door with the grilled peep-hole and the barred-and-shuttered windows through which no light shone.

Ed knew THE THIRTEEN CLUB pretty well; he had a card of admission to it, had often visited it when his vaudeville bookings brought him to New York. It was a pretty swank place, and its exterior gave no hint of the huge sums of money that were won and lost every night across the poker tables. Ed had never been able to find out who operated the Club, but he knew that, whoever it was, the proprietor must be pretty clever. No roulette wheels, no dice tables that had to be camouflaged in the event of a raid. Poker was a gentleman's game, and here, only poker was played. The chips might represent pennies, dollars or centuries, but no money was ever exhibited at the tables. The police had long ago given up as a bad job the proposition of trying to get the goods on THE THIRTEEN CLUB....

Nevertheless, fortunes had been won and lost there, men had been ruined in that poker game.

Ed went there occasionally when he couldn't find anything more exciting. He was known on the vaudeville stage as THE MASKED MARKSMAN, and under that stage name he had taken the country by storm, packing the houses wherever he appeared. His specialty was an acrobatic juggling number, using heavy .45 caliber revolvers similar to the two which he now carried in his armpit holsters, instead of the usual dumbbells that were the concomitants of the average juggling act. The feats of marksmanship which he performed on the stage while juggling those revolvers were little short of miraculous. He was billed: THE MAN WHO CAN MAKE GUNS TALK!

But he craved excitement, thrills, danger. So he dabbled in crime investigation on the side. He now had licenses to operate as a private detective in a dozen States, and he had chalked up some remarkable successes to his credit in the past few years. Little by little, it become known in the theatrical world that Ed Race could be depended upon to get you out of a jam, if you ever found yourself behind the eight ball. And it was just such a mission that brought Ed Race down here, walking past THE THIRTEEN CLUB this evening.

He didn't stop at the entrance, but went on up the street, rounded the corner.

Joe Dunstan and Norma Maitland were waiting for him in Dunstan's expensive, high-powered sedan, parked at the curb a few feet down from the corner.

Norma Maitland had 'phoned Ed a half hour ago, asking him to meet them around the corner from THE THIRTEEN CLUB. It was urgent, she said.

Ed had known Norma Maitland for years now, and took an almost fatherly interest in her. She was pretty, in a healthy, blond sort of way. Her softly modulated, deep-throated contralto voice had won her headline prominence in the vaudeville circuit, and she had appeared on many bills together with Ed. Now she was in trouble, apparently, and Ed hadn't hesitated to come the minute she called.

Joe Dunstan, who had been sitting behind the wheel beside Norma, got out and shook hands with Ed. He said: "It's damn nice of you to come, Race. I wanted to handle this myself, but Norma insisted."

Ed grunted, said: "You know I'd have been sore if you hadn't let me come. What's it all about?"

Norma Maitland was twisting a handkerchief in her hands. "It's about my brother, Harry. I—I'm afraid he's gotten himself into a terrible spot."

Dunstan put a hand on her shoulder, said soothingly: "Let me tell him, Norma."

She pecked at her eyes with the handkerchief, said huskily: "All right, Joe."

Dunstan turned to Ed. "Look, Race. You know I want to marry Norma. I've been trying for three years now, and she hasn't made up her mind yet. Well, considering that she will, eventually, naturally I look on Harry almost as my brother-in-law. You know he works in the Gerard Bank. Well, I'll put it brutally—he's embezzled forty thousand dollars—and every nickel of it he's lost in THE THIRTEEN CLUB around the corner here!"

Ed whistled. "Forty grand! That's a hell of a lot of dough!"

"Sure it is," Dunstan went on eagerly, "but not to me. I could pay it out and I wouldn't miss it. I want Norma to let me make it good for Harry, but she won't allow it. You've known her a long time, Race. Tell her it's all right."

Ed looked puzzled. "Let me get this straight, Joe. Why did you have me meet you here?"

Norma said brokenly: "Because Harry's in there now!" She turned away from him suddenly, covered her face with her hands.

Dunstan started to put an arm around her shoulders

27

consolingly, but Ed yanked him by the sleeve, said: "Let her cry, Joe. It'll do her good. You can tell me all about this business. What's Harry doing in there now?"

Joe Dunstan led him away a few feet, out of Norma's hearing. "I was over at Norma's house this evening, and Harry came in. He looked all wrought up, and his face was flushed and excited. They went in the next room, but Harry talked so loud I couldn't help hearing everything he said. Norma hadn't suspected a thing before. Harry told her about the forty thousand he'd embezzled and lost there, and then—" Dunstan paused, lowered his voice even more—"he told her he had thirty thousand more in his pocket that he'd taken today. He was going down to THE THIRTEEN CLUB and make one last try to recoup. And if he didn't, he said he was going to blow his brains out. The reason why he was telling her about it, was because he wanted her to use the proceeds of his insurance money to reimburse the Gerard Bank!"

Ed said thoughtfully: "Harry's only a kid. He hasn't got a chance with the sharks that play there—even if the game's on the level. And I'm pretty sure THE THIRTEEN CLUB doesn't make its profit on percentage alone."

"That's what I say!" Dunstan exclaimed eagerly. "They'll take the thirty thousand away from him, too, and he'll bump himself off!"

"The way I get it," Ed ruminated, "it's my job to go in there and take him out."

Norma had stopped sobbing. She had come up to them now, and she put an impulsive hand on Ed's arm. "Would you, Ed?"

Ed smiled. "Of course I will, Norma."

"And then," Joe Dunstan broke in, "I want Norma to let me make up Harry's shortage."

Norma Maitland looked pleadingly at Dunstan. "Please, Joe, don't insist on that. I—I couldn't let you—"

She stopped as a maroon limousine with a plug-ugly chauffeur, and two men in the rear, sped past them, rounded the corner toward The Thirteen Club. The thing that had attracted her attention was the fact that one of the two men in the interior had been leaning forward, staring at them out of the window. His face was long and sallow under a black slouch hat; his mouth was a thin gash of cold cruelty.

She shuddered. "That man—he stared at me so queerly—"

"I know him," Ed muttered. "He's Nick Savoldi, manager of the Club; just a figurehead for the real owner, but supposed to be pretty tough all by himself. I think I'll go in and have a talk with Nick."

"Wait," Joe Dunstan broke in thoughtfully. "I know Nick, too. I've been in the place myself, and I once did Savoldi a favor." He glanced at Ed deprecatingly. "You'd only shoot the place up, perhaps get yourself in a jam, and bring the cops down. We can't afford that—Harry might be picked up, and his shortage exposed before we could cover it."

Ed shrugged. "What do you suggest, Joe?"

"Let me go in first, Race. Maybe I can do more with Savoldi—you know—'A kind word turneth away wrath.' If I don't come out in, say, a half hour, you come in after me. Got a membership card?"

Ed nodded. "Go ahead."

He watched Dunstan leave them, turn the corner. Norma Maitland gripped his arm. "Oh, Ed, I appreciate everything Joe is doing, but I'd rather you could have taken care of it. If Joe puts up that money, gets Harry out of this jam, I—I'll feel—obligated—"

"You mean you'll have to marry him?"

"Y-yes."

"And you'd rather not?"

"I—I don't know, Ed. Joe's nice; he's been awfully attentive, and all that. But, somehow, I don't think I could give up the vaudeville stage." She turned her gaze toward him. "*You* know how I feel, Ed. You're a trouper yourself."

Ed Race pressed her arm, smiled a slow smile of understanding. "It gets in your blood, doesn't it, Norma? I—"

From around the corner came a mad outcry, the thud of a fist against flesh and bone, the wild scream of a youth: "Damn you, damn you! Let me in again. Give me a chance!"

Norma Maitland's eyes widened in terrified surprise. "That's Harry. I know his voice!"

Ed was already speeding around the corner. The sight that met his eyes was not an unusual one. It was the spectacle of an inebriated youth being bounced from a more or less exclusive establishment where he had made a nuisance of himself.

The youth was Harry Maitland. And the door of The thirteen Club was just closing on the gaunt visage of Nick Savoldi, who had apparently participated in the bouncing.

Harry Maitland lay on the sidewalk, stirring weakly. Beside him stood the thug whom Ed Race had seen in the limousine with Savoldi. He had a square face and a flat nose, looked as if he might at one time have been a second-rate boxer. His knuckles were gnarled and twisted.

At the moment, however, he wasn't using his knuckles; he was directing a vicious kick at the limp body of Harry Maitland. The kick landed in young Maitland's ribs, tearing the breath out of the lad, leaving him white and gasping on the ground.

Ed reached the thug's side, swung his left fist up in a short, compact arc that landed flush on the other's chin, rocked him backward, and sent him sprawling against the wall of THE THIR-TEEN CLUB.

The blow had been a hard one, delivered with the impetus of Ed's run added to the weight of his body and the heft of his broad shoulders. Ed had meant it to be a knockout, hadn't cared if it did a whole lot of harm. He had seen that vicious kick.

But the thug was used to taking them on the chin. He reeled, splayed his hands out against the wall for support, and glared at Ed. Then his hand went for a gun. He was fast, but compared to the swift, lightning-like motion of Ed's hand, he resembled a snail. Ed had practiced that draw for years, performed it every night on the stage.

As if by legerdemain, one of his heavy forty-five caliber revolvers seemed to have materialized out of thin air.

Ed swept it up in a swift motion, struck the thug's wrist with the barrel while his ham-like paw was still reaching into his breast pocket. There was the sound of snapping bone, and the thug dropped his arm, the hand hanging limp, his face suddenly twisted, sweating with the pain of a broken wrist.

31

Ed grinned thinly, stepped back a pace so that he stood over Harry Maitland. He kept his revolver leveled, still covering the thug, growled out of the corner of his mouth to the boy: "You all right, Harry? Can you get up?"

Young Maitland groaned, managed to struggle to his feet. He murmured weakly:

"Ed! Those guys trimmed me, threw me out. My God, I had thirty thousand dollars, and I dropped all but five hundred. They wouldn't let me play any more, wouldn't give me a chance—"

"Shut up!" Ed snapped, still keeping his eyes on the thug, who was holding his injured wrist with his other hand, glaring murderously.

"What's your name, gorilla?" Ed asked him.

"Go to hell! I'll have your hide for this!"

"His name is Louie, Ed," the boy spoke up. "That's the name I know him by. He's Nick Savoldi's bodyguard."

"What happened to Joe Dunstan?" Ed asked. "He went in there after you a few minutes ago."

"Joe is there, arguing with Savoldi. But Savoldi wouldn't listen to him. He ordered me thrown out anyway."

Ed's lips tightened, his eyes grew grim. "All right, Louie," he rapped out at the gorilla, "we're all going inside. I guess I better talk to your boss."

Louie's eyes narrowed, his teeth showed in a snarl. "That's what *you* say. Try and get in, Wise Guy!"

Ed grinned wickedly. He stepped close, whispered softly: "Look, Louie. I happen to know that the cop on this beat stays away from here all night. Your big boss, whoever he is, sees to it that he keeps at the far end of the beat."

Louie winced from the pain of his wrist, scowled. "So what, Wise Guy?"

"So there'll be nobody at all to interfere with what I'm going to do to you, pal."

He raised the revolver above the other's head. "Did you ever have your face side-swiped with the barrel of a forty-five? It hurts like hell. I can cut your map to ribbons—so it'll look like the map of Europe after the War. And that's just what I'm going to do in one minute, if you don't be a good Boy Scout, and follow orders!"

Ed stopped talking, stood tense in front of the hood, with the heavy revolver poised. His calm, cold gray eyes met those of the other, their glances locked. The cold, purposeful stare of those eyes of Ed's convinced the man he would do just what he promised.

He glanced from Ed to the Maitland boy, who stood just behind him, then back to Ed again. He licked his lips, looked up fearfully at the gun barrel, lowered his eyes, and asked: "What— you want me to do?"

Ed grinned. "That's better. You're going to ring the bell of this place, and I'm going to stand to one side. When the doorman opens the grill, you'll tell him everything is jake, you've got rid of the kid, and to let you in. Then when he opens the door, I'll come in with you. After that you can stay or scram—it's all the same to me. But I advise you to scram."

Louie licked his lips again. "Savoldi seen you around the

corner with that dame. He gave strict orders not to let you in. He'd have my hide—"

"The minute is up," Ed told him coldly. His arm, which held the revolver, stiffened.

"Wait!" Louie cried, frightened. "Don't slash me, mister. I'll do it!"

Ed nodded. "You're smart."

He sidestepped, dragged the boy along with him. His eye caught sight of Norma Maitland, standing anxiously near the corner. She had been watching the tableau tensely. Now she came running over, folded her brother in her arms. "Harry, Harry. Are you hurt?"

The boy twisted out of her embrace, his handsome young features contorted into a sullen expression. "Didn't I tell you not to mix in this, Norma? You'll only get Ed and Joe in trouble. Savoldi's in there, and he's a killer. You should've left me alone!"

Ed kept his eyes on Louie, said over his shoulder, "Give me that five hundred you have left, Harry."

"What for?"

"Give it to me, quick!"

Under that whiplash command the boy's sullenness faded. He produced a roll of bills from his pocket, handed them over.

"Now," Ed ordered the girl, "take your brother away from here, Norma. I'm going in there and see what's happened to Joe; also to see what I can do with Savoldi."

But Norma Maitland surprised him. "We're *not* going away, Ed! Harry and I aren't going to let you and Joe fight our battles for us alone. We're going in with you!"

Ed recognized that tone. There was no use arguing with Norma Maitland when she got stubborn—and they didn't have all night, either. He shrugged, said: "Have it your way, Norma."

He said to Louie: "All right, gorilla. Ring the bell!"

He drew Norma and the boy close to the wall, while Louie, under the threat of the revolver, put his finger on the button just below the metal plaque which bore the name of the club.

Somewhere inside, a bell jangled. In a moment, the little grilled peephole opened; an eye stared out.

Louie hesitated, and Ed poked him in the side with the gun. Louie said: "It's all right, Tiny. I got rid of the kid. Let's get in."

There was a grunt, the peephole closed, and the heavy door swung open. Ed stepped quickly into the doorway, slamming into Louie with his shoulder so as to send him sprawling on the sidewalk. He stood aside while Norma and her brother ran in past him. Then he entered the vestibule, closed the door behind him.

A big man, who must have weighed all of two hundred and ten pounds, stared at them out of little pin point eyes that were almost buried in folds of fat. His triple chin wagged in astonishment.

"What the hell's this?"

He didn't have time to ask any more, because Ed moved close, clubbing his revolver. He said: "It's all about this, Tiny," and brought the leaded butt down on the fat man's temple in a smashing blow.

Tiny's eyes disappeared entirely, his mouth dropped open, letting his chins sag. He collapsed gently to the floor.

Ed motioned Norma and Harry to follow him, stepped through the vestibule into a wide foyer. The floor was carpeted with an expensive hooked rug that must have cost at least a thousand dollars. The place was furnished handsomely and lavishly. Apparently the owner had no fear of a police raid, for he had put plenty of money into the place.

To the left, a staircase led upward. Ed said to Norma over his shoulder: "Upstairs is where they play. Savoldi's office is down here. You wait—"

He stopped short as a door further down in the hall, which led off the foyer, opened abruptly.

Nick Savoldi appeared, started to walk in their direction, toward the staircase. Before he had taken more than two steps, he saw Ed, with Norma and Harry. He jerked to a stop; his hand flashed toward his armpit.

But Ed covered him with the big forty-five. "Hold it just like that, Savoldi!"

Savoldi's gaunt face betrayed nothing of his thoughts. Only his eyes burned intensely. He glanced at Harry Maitland, then looked back at Ed. "What's the trouble, Mr. Race?" he asked innocently.

Ed advanced along the hall, holding the gun level. He said: "Back up into your room again, Nick."

Savoldi said: "Sure, sure, Mr. Race. But you don't need that gun. What's the big idea?"

He was backing into the room even as he talked. Ed's revolver was poking into his chest. Norma and Harry followed them in, and Norma shut the door.

Savoldi's office had a row of filing cabinets against one wall, a door which connected with the next room on the opposite wall. Near the window was a rich mahogany desk upon which rested a typewriter and two telephones. Ed knew that one of these was an outside wire; the other was the house 'phone.

Savoldi backed up to his desk, leaned against it, and wheezed: "But I don't understand, Mr. Race—"

"What's happened to Joe Dunstan?" Ed demanded.

Savoldi shrugged. "We—er—had a little argument. He left in a huff."

"I was in the street all the time," Ed grated, "and I didn't see him come out."

Savoldi smiled broadly, shrugged. "We have more than one entrance, as you your self know, Mr. Race. But—"

"All right. Let that rest. Let's talk about Harry Maitland, here. The kid's a good friend of mine. He dropped seventy grand here in the past few weeks, and he's in one hell of a jam."

There was a nasty flicker in Savoldi's eyes. His upper lip quirked in a half sneer. "That is not my fault, Mr. Race. We cannot wet-nurse our clients. The young man insisted upon playing in the game with the five-hundred-dollar chips, and he had the money—so what were we going to do?"

Ed whistled. "Five-hundred-buck chips!"

He glanced sideways at Harry Maitland, who lowered his eyes. "I'm sorry, Ed," the boy whispered. "I was a damn' fool." He raised his head, thrust out his chin. "But I'll take my medicine. There's nothing you can do to help me. I lost the money gambling, and I wouldn't take it back even if Savoldi wanted to give it to me."

Norma put a hand on her brother's shoulder. "I—I think I know where I can get the money for you to make up your shortage, Harry. Let's get out of here—" Her voice broke.

Ed put his gun away. "I'm sorry I barged in in this way, Savoldi. I guess you're right. The kid played and lost. You're not in business for your health."

Savoldi relaxed slightly at sight of the disappearing gun. He said more eagerly: "It's all right, Mr. Race. Many of us go off the handle that way. I'm sorry the boy was treated so rough before, but Louie had to put him out. He was raising too much of a disturbance, and you know how quiet this place is ordinarily."

Savoldi went to the door, held it open for them. "I wish there was something I could do," he went on glibly, "but you know I'm not the boss. And I couldn't give Mr. Maitland seventy grand out of my own pocket. I only work here on a salary."

Ed suddenly snapped his fingers. "Wait a minute. I've got a hunch."

He strode across to the desk, drew a checkbook from his pocket, and wrote out a check for five thousand dollars. He thrust it at Savoldi.

"I'm going to take a whirl at the poker table. Give me chips for that—five hundred dollar ones!"

Savoldi took the check hesitantly. "You—never played that high before, Mr. Race."

"I'm doing it now."

"Well—"

"Well, what? Are you afraid of the check?"

"Oh, no, Mr. Race, not at all. Your check is good here any day. Savoldi shrugged. "It's okay with me, Mr. Race."

He went around to the front of the desk, took a steel strongbox out of the top drawer, and from it extracted ten yellow, metal chips which he handed to Ed.

"There you are, sir. Five thousand dollars. I'm afraid it won't go far in that game though."

Ed took the chips without saying anything, turned to Norma and Harry Maitland. "You stay down here, Norma. Women aren't allowed upstairs. You, Harry, come up with me. You're going to watch behind my chair while I play, and see that nothing is pulled off."

Before Savoldi or Norma could say anything, Ed had pushed Harry Maitland out of the room, rushed him upstairs.

There were five or six rooms on the upper floor. Ed was familiar with the layout. One room was a combination rest and smoking room, with checkerboards and a ping-pong table. Recently a bar had been installed there, and members could get anything they wanted to eat or drink without paying a cent. In the other rooms there were always games going on, and you could pick your own stakes. There was a game with fifty-cent chips, one with dollar and two-dollar chips, another where the smallest chips were fifty-dollar denomination, and then the fourth room, where only the elite played, with five-hundred-dollar chips. You had to go through the barroom to get to all the games.

The bartender raised his eyebrows in astonishment as he saw Ed and Harry Maitland make for the door of the last room.

"Excuse me, Mr. Race," he called out.

"That's the five hundred"

"It's all right, Sam," Ed told him. "We're taking a special fling tonight."

Ed opened the door, pushed Harry Maitland through. Four men were sitting around a table, tense, tight-lipped. A house dealer was distributing cards. There was an air of quiet tension in this room, and no conversation was made except for the purposefully monotonous tones of the players in announcing their bets.

Ed knew two of the four players. They were professional gamblers of not too savory reputation. Their names were Farrell and Buckner. The other two, though Ed had seen them around town, were unknown to him by name. They were the playboy type, evidently wealthy suckers; and it was apparent that Farrell and Buckner were finding them easy prey, judging by their stacks of chips.

Ed had no doubt that the two gamblers were working under some sort of tacit arrangement whereby they split their profits with the house.

Farrell looked up from his cards, said: "Oh, hello, Maitland! You back?" Then he saw Ed, exclaimed: "Well, Mr. Race! You joining us big-timers?"

Ed pulled up a chair between Farrell and Buckner, who spread out to make room for him. "If you don't mind," he said pleasantly. "I feel lucky tonight."

Farrell introduced him to the other two men. "Meet—er— Mr. Smith and Mr. Jones." He grinned. "Names don't mean anything here. The fact that we're allowed to play means that we're okay."

Ed put his chips on the table, and the house man dealt him in. "We're playing open blind," Farrell told him. "Blind opener can buy four cards, and re-raise."

Ed nodded. "Okay by me." He noted that "Mr. Smith and Mr. Jones" were a bit nervous, sitting in strained attitudes. Both had long glasses of whiskey-and-soda beside them, from which they drank.

Buckner was first, and opened blind for five hundred, throwing in his chip carelessly. Mr. Smith stayed, after studying his cards carefully, and Mr. Jones dropped out. Buckner was next. He squeezed his cards, squinted at them, and threw in two chips. "Up five hundred!" he said laconically.

Ed had already looked at his cards. He had three aces. "All the cards in the game?" he asked.

"No, sir," the dealer told him. "Sorry I didn't mention it before. The two's, three's and four's are out."

Ed saw Buckner's raise, put in two chips. With the two's, three's and four's out, three aces wouldn't be a top hand. The cards generally ran high when the low ones were out, and Buckner might have a straight on the go. However, three aces had to be played.

Farrell pushed in two chips.

"I'll raise it again," he said carelessly.

Mr. Smith looked troubled, but put in his two chips. Buckner said pleasantly: "Sorry, but it'll cost you another chip. I'm re-raising."

Ed's eyes narrowed. He recognized the stunt. He and Smith were sandwiched in between these two professionals, who were boosting the pot to make a killing.

He said nothing, though, saw the two raises, watched Farrell and Smith put their money in.

Buckner grinned. "Well, I guess it's a real pot now. Let's buy cards."

Farrell said: "I'll take three."

Ed frowned. "You had your nerve re-raising on a pair."

Farrell shrugged. "Buckner's bluffing. He probably hasn't got a thing."

Mr. Smith drew two cards, and Ed figured him for three of a kind, or else he wouldn't have stayed. Ed's aces were better than Smith's holding.

The dealer looked inquiringly at Buckner, who said: "I just want one card."

Ed's eyes swiveled to the dealer just in time to see him slip a card from the bottom of the deck.

The movement of Ed's hand was so swift that it took them all by surprise. It clamped tightly over the dealer's wrist, gripping it cruelly, holding him so that the bottom card was half in and half out of the deck. The dealer was caught cold.

"Well," Ed said softly, "this explains a lot." He twisted the dealer's wrist so that the card fell to the table. It was the king of spades.

The dealer's face was white, his eyes searching in every direction for escape. Ed let him go, swung on Buckner. "Let's see your cards!" he ordered.

Buckner glared at him. "I demand the pot!" he spluttered. "You broke it up when I was winning! I—"

Ed reached up, gripped him by the lapel of his coat. "Are you going to show me those cards?" he asked.

"Let go of me!" Buckner rasped. Then he raised his voice, shouted: "Nick! Help!"

He got no further. Ed's fist came up in a flashing blow that caught him on the chin, lifted him from the floor. In the same instant Ed sidestepped, whirled, his left hand darting to his armpit holster. It came out with one of the forty-fives, and he stood there smiling coldly, covering Farrell and the dealer. The dealer hadn't moved, but Farrell was raising a small automatic which had come out of his pocket.

Farrell's jaw dropped open as he realized he was staring into the muzzle of a forty-five caliber revolver, less than a foot from his face. He let go of the automatic, allowed it to drop to the floor, and shouted: "Don't shoot!"

Ed grinned, stooped and picked up the automatic, which he pocketed. He threw a glance toward the door, where young Maitland was standing. "Lock the door, Harry," he ordered.

He didn't wait to see that he was obeyed, but walked around and frisked the dealer, who submitted meekly. Ed took from his hip pocket a small twenty-two caliber pistol.

Then he backed away, bent beside Buckner, and picked up the five cards which the gambler had dropped when he was knocked out.

Ed laid them on the table, face up, and said to Mr. Smith and Mr. Jones: "That'll show you how your money went."

The five cards consisted of three kings, a jack and a nine.

"Buckner was buying only one card," Ed explained to them. "Ordinarily nobody would keep a jack for a heeler. But Buckner knew what he was going to buy; he knew he'd get a fourth king. I'd probably have got a full house, aces up, and he expected me to bet my head off against his four kings!"

Mr. Smith glared at Farrell and the dealer. Jones exploded: "Thirty grand I've dropped here in the last few months—in this *gentleman's* game! I want my money back!"

Farrell shrank from the table, glanced at the dealer. The dealer cleared his throat, said cautiously: "Look, Mr. Race—maybe if we go down and see Nick, he will square things up. I did wrong, but I had to deal 'em like that, or I'd be out of a job. I think you can make Nick pony up."

Ed nodded grimly. "You bet I'll make Nick pony up. Let's go." He motioned toward the door. "And don't try anything. I feel a little sore."

Harry Maitland unlocked the door, and they filed out, Farrell and the dealer first, then Mr. Smith and Mr. Jones. Ed pushed Harry out next, then followed, leaving Buckner still out on the floor.

The barroom was deserted; the bartender gone. Harry Maitland whispered: "He must have heard the ruckus, and gone down to warn Nick."

Ed said nothing, shepherded his company down to the ground floor and into Nick's office.

Norma Maitland wasn't there. But Nick Savoldi was, with the bartender. Neither had a gun. The bartender was standing beside Nick's desk, and Nick was sitting quietly, his hands on the glass top.

He spoke quickly, before Ed had a chance to say anything. "I think we can fix this up, Mr. Race. These clucks should have known enough to lay off while you were in the game."

Ed closed the door behind him, stood with his back to it. He looked at Mr. Jones. "How much have *you* lost in this place?"

Mr. Jones answered promptly. "Twelve thousand, three hundred dollars. I ought to get interest on it, too!"

"Okay," said Ed. He swung on Savoldi. "That's twenty for Smith, twelve-three for Jones, and a hundred thousand even thousand, three hundred."

Nick smiled ingratiatingly. "If you'll wait just a few minutes, I think I can fix for Harry Maitland. A hundred and thirty everything up."

"Where's Miss Maitland?" Ed asked.

"She—er—left, Mr. Race. "She—"

Ed took a long step over to the desk, elbowed the bartender out of the way. *"Where's Miss Maitland?"* he repeated. "I'll give you one minute to tell me what you've done with her!"

Savoldi gulped, said very low: "She's in the next room." He jerked his head toward the connecting door at the left. "With the boss."

Ed whirled, handed his revolver to Harry Maitland. "Cover these birds," he rapped. "And look out for the trigger; it goes off if you touch it."

He turned, started for the connecting door. Just then it

opened a crack, and the muzzle of a gun was stuck out. An eye appeared at the crack behind the gun.

Ed stopped short in mid-stride. He was close to Farrell. He gripped the gambler by the arm, hurled him at the crack in the door just as the gun spat. Farrell uttered a scream, staggered backward with a bullet in his shoulder.

In that second, Ed had drawn his second revolver from the other shoulder holster. The room rocked to the heavy explosion of the big forty-five. The gun disappeared from the crack in the door, as did the eye behind it.

Nick Savoldi started up from behind the desk, shouting: "He's killed the boss!" Nick reached into the open drawer beside him, but Harry Maitland yelled: "Sit still, Savoldi!"

Nick dropped back into the chair, took his hand away from the drawer. He glared at young Maitland.

Ed grinned, said: "Good stuff, Harry. Hold 'em like that," and sprang through the connecting door. A body lay in the next room on the floor, close to the door, face down.

Norma Maitland lay on a couch at the far end. She had been gagged and blindfolded, and her hands tied behind her. She was struggling, kicking desperately.

Ed sprang over the body on the floor, untied her bonds. She sat up, smiled. "You took an awful long time, Ed," she said.

He helped her up, then walked over to the body of the man he had shot, turned it over. Norma uttered a gasp. "Joe Dunstan!" she exclaimed.

"That's right," Ed said bitterly. "He was the real boss of THE THIRTEEN CLUB. He planned to get your brother in a hole, and then help him out with the money he took from the kid in his crooked game. That's how he figured on getting you to marry him!"

He took her by the arm, led her into the next room. "Your boss is dead, Nick," he informed Savoldi. "You've got nobody to protect you with the cops any more. When they get here it's going to be pretty hot for you."

Savoldi's face had gone a pasty yellow.

"You could make it easier for yourself."

"How?" Savoldi asked hoarsely.

"By opening up that safe in back of you, and reimbursing these gentlemen."

Savoldi got up from the desk. "I'll do it, Mr. Race," he said. "You—you'll put in a good word for me, won't you? You stand in well with the department."

"I'll do that," Ed promised.

He watched grimly while Savoldi opened the safe, took out a huge stack of currency, and began counting it out.

Norma Maitland looked up at him with wet eyes. "Ed," she murmured, "You're a darling!"

Ed grinned down at her, patted her on the back. "Don't mention it to a soul!"

CUE FOR A GUNMAN

I T WAS about eleven o'clock in the morning when Leon Partages laid the five thousand dollars on the nose for *Gray Mama* to win the Preakness at Pimlico. It was in Kelty's restaurant on Broadway, and Ed Race had just come in for a late Sunday breakfast. Ed had nothing to do for the day except to appear in a Milk Fund Benefit along about midnight. He was looking for a little something in the way of excitement—and he found it.

He saw Leon Partages at a table in the far corner, counting a lot of cash across the table to Nick Slingel, the bookmaker. Ed didn't like Slingel at all, but he liked Partages a lot—not because the fat, shrewd, good-natured Leon was the boss of the vaudeville circuit for which he worked, but because he had developed a real affection for the man.

Ed crossed over to the table, kicked out a chair, and sat down. Partages looked up, said: "Hello, Eddie boy. Be through in just a minute." He went on thumbing out fifty-dollar bills. "Forty-five-fifty, forty-six hundred, forty-six-fifty—"

Ed glanced at Slingel, frowned. The bookie looked at him guilelessly out of his small, closely set eyes. He grinned crookedly. "Leon's got a hot one for the Preakness, Race. If she comes in, it'll send me to the poorhouse; I'm givin' him fifty to one."

Partages finished counting, pushed the pile of money over to

Slingel. "There you are, Nick—five grand at fifty to one on *Gray Mama* on the nose in the Preakness."

Slingel grinned, pocketed the money, and scribbled something on a slip of paper. "There's your memorandum, in case you win!" He arose to go, but Partages stopped him.

"Wait a minute, Nick, maybe I'll let Eddie in on this." He turned to Ed. "Look, boy, this is a hot tip that I got from a bum on the bowery that I staked to a handout. I gave him a buck, and he says: 'Thanks, mister, you're a white guy. I'm gonna do something for you—I'm gonna give you the name of the winning horse in the Preakness today.' And he named this here *Gray Mama*. So I'm laying five grand on her!"

Ed sighed. "My God, Mr. Partages, do you mean to say that you're risking five thousand dollars on the word of a Bowery bum?"

"That's right," Partages assured him. "I've come through all my life, playing hunches, and this is one of them. You take a tip from me, and get in on this. Say the word, and I'll put up a thousand for you."

"No, thanks," Ed said. He glared at Slingel. "You ought to be ashamed of yourself, letting Leon make a bet like that."

Slingel shrugged. "If it wasn't for guys like him, this would be a lousy business, Race. Look at the odds I'm laying him."

"If you pay off," Ed said sourly.

Slingel's face darkened. For a moment he looked almost dangerous. His mouth twisted nastily. "If anybody but you made that crack, Race—"

"Forget it," Ed told him. "Only if Mr. Partages wins, you better see that you *do* pay off."

When Slingel had gone, Partages turned a troubled face to Ed. "What did you mean by that, Eddie boy, about his paying off? It's not like you to insult a man without cause."

Ed toyed with a knife, muttered moodily: "There's a rumor going around, Mr. Partages, about Lou Donegan. Remember—he was found in the river with his throat slit?"

Partages nodded. "I sure do! And they never found the skunks that did it."

"No," Ed agreed slowly. "But the rumor goes that Lou Donegan had made a cleanup at the track—and that Slingel was the bookie who had to do the paying off. Only Donegan wasn't alive to collect."

Partages let out a long sigh. "God! Would he kill a man like Lou Donegan to save himself some lousy money?"

ED SHRUGGED. "I don't know." He suddenly put a hand on the other's shoulder. "Only I want you to promise me something, Mr. Partages. If, by some freak of chance, *Gray Mama* should win this afternoon, you call me, and let me hang around with you till after Slingel pays off!"

That was at eleven; at six-thirty Ed got back to the Longmont, where he was staying, and picked up a newspaper at the stand in the lobby on the way up to his room for a quick shower before supper. It was a sporting final, and the black headline at the left-hand side of the page almost took him off his feet:

DARK HORSE WINS PREAKNESS PURSE

Gray Mama lopes in ahead of the track at odds of fifty to one

Ed was in the elevator when he read it, and he swore softly under his breath.

"What's the matter, Mr. Race?" the operator asked. "Bad news?"

"It sounds like good news, Al," Ed told him, "but there's no telling how it'll turn out. A friend of mine just made a quarter of a million dollars!"

Al whistled. "Boy, that don't sound bad, Mr. Race. I wish he was a friend of mine."

When Ed got in his room he didn't bother about the shower.

He 'phoned Partages' home. The vaudeville owner's daughter got on the wire.

"Where's your dad, Elsie?" Ed demanded without preamble.

"He's gone to meet a man by the name of Slingel," Elsie Partages told him. "Didn't you hear about Dad's horse winning the Preakness? Dad had five thousand dollars on *Gray Mama*, and it came in first. I'm going to get a present of a brand-new racing yacht. Isn't that lovely? I—"

"Listen," Eddie broke in, "never mind about the yacht. Do you know where your father went to meet Slingel? He promised to call me."

"He did, Ed, but you hadn't got back to the hotel yet, and Mr. Slingel insisted on meeting him right away so he could pay him; so dad didn't bother to leave a message for you. He took a cab to Mr. Slingel's office on Forty-ninth Street."

"See you later, Elsie," Ed told her hastily, and hung up.

He kept his finger on the elevator button until the cage came up, and then made Al ride him all the way down without stopping. The Longmont was on Forty-third, and it was quicker to walk than to take a cab through the congested Broadway traffic.

Ed pushed through the crowds, bleak-eyed. He knew enough about Slingel to know that he wouldn't pay off two hundred and fifty thousand dollars without batting an eyelash. Slingel had pulled many a fast one in the past, and there were any number of killers in the city whom he could hire for a thousand dollars for any kind of job from murder down.

Slingel was reputed to be worth four or five million in cold cash, which he kept distributed in a dozen safe-deposit boxes throughout the city. In addition to his bookmaking, he lent out money at usurious interest, and enforced repayment with the threat of his hired killers. It was whispered about that in those deposit boxes, besides cash, there were signed promissory notes from judges, district attorneys and many other men prominent in city, state and national affairs.

There were plenty of people who hated Slingel, but he remained alive mainly because his death would have caused disgrace or worse to so many influential persons.

Ed Race himself had nothing to worry about on that score. He had always lived the simple life, even though he knew the Great White Way intimately. An acrobatic juggler by profession, he had made enough money in his eight years on the stage to have retired comfortably, if he had saved it.

HE HAD blazed a name on the vaudeville circuits from coast to coast, appearing as the "Masked Marksman." His specialty had no rival on the stage. He performed his feats of juggling not with clubs or trick weights, but with real, honest-to-goodness forty-five caliber revolvers, similar to the two which he now carried in the twin holsters under his armpits.

He had so mastered those six-guns of his that he performed almost incredible feats of marksmanship with them—feats that left the audience breathless with admiration.

But with all that, he found that his nervous system craved continuous excitement. The few minutes each day that he spent behind the footlights left him plenty of leisure; and in that leisure he had developed the hobby that gave him the additional quota of excitement he needed—he played around with criminology. He now had licenses to operate as a private detective in a dozen states, and he had earned the praise of numerous police officials as well as the hatred of many criminals.

Slingel, he knew, hated him; hated him in a malicious, envious way.

Slingel envied Ed's superb physique, his superlatively trained muscles that responded automatically to each impulse from his brain. Daily practice on the stage had developed a perfect coördination between mind and muscle that had got him out of many a tight spot where instant action—of the right kind—was the only barrier between life and death.

Now, as Ed Race turned the corner from Broadway into Forty-ninth, he saw the three-story brownstone building which Slingel used as an office and occasional residence. The front of the ground floor had been converted into a single, large, plate-glass window bearing in gilt letters the legend:

NICHOLAS SLINGEL CO., INC.
REAL ESTATE & INSURANCE
BAIL BONDS

Slingel wrote bail bonds for all the major underworld characters, and charged them exorbitant fees. His insurance business was tremendous—enough to have satisfied any legitimate businessman—but it was only chicken-feed to Slingel.

Ed saw a light behind the plate-glass window and started to cross the street toward the office. But two things happened at almost the same time....

A tall man and a short man came out of the brownstone

building. The taller one was carrying a small Boston bag that seemed very full. They walked swiftly to the curb, entered a black sedan that was waiting for them with the motor running.

Ed's eyes narrowed, and he hastened his step. He knew both of those men. The tall one was Manny Sloss, and the short one was Joe Ricci. They were two of the "boys." Ed knew that they were on Slingel's payroll, and so did the police. But no one had ever been able to get anything on either of them. They literally got away with murder.

From their tense attitude as they crossed to the sedan, Ed knew that they were getting away with something right now. He started toward them but hadn't taken more than two steps off the curb when the second thing happened; something hard was poked into the small of his back, and a voice said:

"Don't look behind you, Race. Just turn around and walk back to Broadway. You're not wanted on this street." An additional jab of the gun emphasized the next words. "Get goin' now!"

Ed's face flushed a dull red. His hands clenched tight, and his whole body was taut as a spring. Deliberately he turned around to face the man who had spoken. At the same time he shouted loudly so that half a dozen passersby heard him:

"Go ahead and shoot, rat! You'll never escape with all these people to identify you! Go ahead, rat! Shoot me, and you'll burn!"

Ed was now facing the other squarely. The man was stocky, pimply complexioned. He was dressed in a light tan suit, and wore a brown felt hat. His chin was long and came to a sharp point under a pair of thick, red lips.

Those lips opened wide now in astonishment mingled with

rage. He had his right hand in his jacket pocket, and the gun bulged there unmistakably, pointing at Ed's stomach.

FOR A moment Ed thought that the man was going to shoot anyway. He glared at Ed, took a short step back as if to give himself room to fire. Ed's body tingled in anticipation of the impact of the slug. He could do nothing about it. A crowd had gathered around them, attracted by Ed's loud cry; a gay, happy crowd that thought this was some new kind of advertising stunt. There were women and a couple of children in that crowd, and Ed was unwilling to endanger their lives. He had to depend on his trick to work.

The gunman's slow-moving intellect finally got the idea that he was in a spot. Here were more than fifty people who could identify him later, if he should pump a stream of slugs from the automatic in his pocket into Ed Race's body. No amount of influence could save him from the chair in the face of such evidence.

Ed took a step closer to him, saying softly: "It's no good, guy. You're paid for a quick job and a safe getaway. Your boss would never be able to drag you out of the hot seat if you used that gun now. Better fade away while the fading is good."

The other wavered. He didn't really know what to do. And in that second, Ed acted. He had edged close enough now.

His left hand streaked out, gripped the gunman's hand which was in his pocket, twisted it downward, tightening at the same time so as to hold the muzzle of the automatic pointing toward the ground.

Ed's right hand swung in a short arc to the gunman's chin;

there was a short, ugly *snap*, the gunman's head jerked backward, and he was lifted from his feet for an instant, only to wilt to the ground with the automatic still unfired.

Ed stepped back, gazed around at the gaping crowd, and smiled.

"Ladies and gentlemen," he said oratorically, "as you may have guessed, my friend here and I are selling something. We have just demonstrated one of the many methods of self-defense described in our new book, 'How to Protect Yourself Against Thugs.' You can see how efficient this method is. Those of you who wish to purchase a copy, please remain here until I get the book out of our car. My friend will come to in a few minutes."

Before anyone could muster up enough courage to stop him, he had pushed through the crowd, which had by now grown enormously, and crossed the street quickly. He entered the house next door to Nick Slingel's office, looked back and saw that he had got away just in time, for a bluecoat was rounding the corner.

Ed went through to the rear of the building, came out in a dirty, littered yard, climbed a fence, and was in the backyard of Slingel's building.

He tried the rear door, found that it opened, and stepped into a dark room. He worked across this without using his flashlight, went through another door, and suddenly heard a scraping sound. He stopped stock-still, his hand close to his left armpit holster. He was in the room behind the front room with the plate-glass window, and it was pitch dark in here.

The scraping sound ceased, and everything was quiet in the room. From out in the street came the sounds of excited people, the sound of the policeman's voice shouting: "Move back there. Get away from him; give him air, will you? His jaw's broken!"

Ed felt along the wall for a switch, and the scraping sound was resumed. This time it was accompanied by weird grunts and gasps.

Ed found the switch, got his revolver out, and snapped on the lights. He stared for a moment at the two men who lay, gagged and bound with wire, on the floor. One was, as Ed had expected, Leon Partages. The other was Nick Slingel!

Ed said: "Good evening, gentlemen. Am I intruding?"

They both glared up at him. They had been gagged with wads of newspaper stuffed into their mouths, covered with their own handkerchiefs, and tied with wire.

ED BENT and untwisted the wire from Partages' mouth, removed the handkerchief and the newspaper. Then while he worked on the theater-owner's wrists, Partages spat out bits of pulpy newsprint, tried to get the taste of ink out of his mouth by rubbing his tongue against his lips.

"Damn it, Eddie," he finally exclaimed, "I've been held up! Robbed! They took my two hundred and fifty thousand that Slingel just paid me!"

"You don't say so, Mr. Partages," Ed said. "Who did it?"

"Damn it, I don't know. There was a tall man and a short man, and they wore some kind of hoods, with slits for eyes, so you couldn't see a bit of their faces. They busted in here just after Nick had given me the money and I'd given him a receipt for it. They tied us up, and cleaned out Nick's safe, too."

Ed clucked sympathetically. He finished with Partages,

turned to Slingel and untied him. Slingel said nothing till he was free; then he stamped around the room, waving his arms to get the circulation back.

"Wait till I get a hold of those bums!" he raved. "I'll put them through the works. They'll wish they'd never been born. They got Leon's dough, and they took half again as much out of my safe!"

He swung on Ed. "You said I don't pay off. Well, I paid off all right—plenty! If I hadn't been so prompt to hand Leon his dough, this would never have happened!"

"Yeah," Ed said dryly. "I see you pay off. Who are the guys that held you up? Don't tell me you don't know them, either."

Slingel stopped pacing, faced Ed. "That's the truth, Race. I don't know who they were. Some hoods from out of town, probably, who were wised up about the amount of dough I keep around. Nobody in this town would have the guts."

Ed stared at him steadily. "Mr. Partages says one was tall and the other was short. How about Sloss and Ricci? They always work together, and it sounds like them."

Slingel guffawed. "Naw. They would never pull anything like that. Besides," he added hastily, "I happen to know where they are tonight. They're at a party down at Giuseppe's Restaurant in the Village. Not a chance of them getting away from the crowd without being noticed."

"I see," Ed said thoughtfully. He silenced Partages, who was about to break in. "By the way, Slingel, what's the name of that pimply faced guy that works for you these days; you know, the stocky guy?"

Slingel looked blank. "I don't know anybody like that, Race."

Ed grinned. "No? That's funny," he lied. "He told me you paid him to watch the street, and if I should show up while you were in here with Mr. Partages, he was to keep me away even if he had to shoot me."

Slingel almost snarled. "He told you that! He's a damn liar. I'll fix that skunk. Where did this happen?"

"Downstairs," Ed told him cheerfully. "By this time he's probably in the hospital. You see, he may be awful tough for your money, but I found out he has a glass jaw!" He added maliciously, enjoying Slingel's discomfiture: "And I expect you'll be having to bail him out when he's discharged from the hospital. They'll be holding him on a Sullivan charge. He had a gun in his pocket when the cop found him."

Slingel exclaimed: "Look here, Race, you got me all wrong. I—"

"Never mind," Ed told him. "You can save all that for some other time. Right now we're in a hurry."

He took the protesting Partages by the arm, piloted him out before Slingel could think of anything further to say. He led him through the back way, made him climb another fence, giving him a boost over. Then he cut through a back yard, negotiated an alley, and brought the theater owner out on Fiftieth Street.

"Look here, Eddie boy," Partages panted, "what's all this about? Where're you rushing me? I just got robbed of two hundred and fifty thousand dollars, and I don't even know who took it. You go and get Slingel sore—"

"If you don't know who took your money, Mr. Partages, you're not as smart as I thought you were," Ed said.

"You mean—Slingel?"

"That's what I mean, all right. I saw Sloss and Ricci coming out of there with a black bag. Slingel probably staged the whole thing. He paid you off first, and then had those two floods come in and take it away from you. To make it look good, he had them take his own money, too. They'll give it all back to him, and he'll pay them five thousand for the job—*your* five thousand. Net loss to Slingel on *Gray Mama*—nothing. Net gain to Leon Partages—*minus* five thousand dollars. Get the idea?"

PARTAGES WIPED the sweat from his forehead. "Look, Eddie boy, you know I'm pretty well off. Two hundred and fifty grand is a lot of money, but I can live without it. Only I hate to think that Slingel put it over on me. The police?"

"Will do you no good, and you know it, Mr. Partages. Slingel will swear that the two men who held you up were *not* Sloss and Ricci. And those hoods will have iron-clad alibis. Didn't Slingel say that they were at a party at Giuseppe's Restaurant? The alibi was all set beforehand. There'll be a dozen people to swear that Sloss and Ricci never left Giuseppe's all evening."

Partages gave that some thought. Finally he said: "Listen, Eddie, can you get that money back?"

"I think so, Mr. Partages, but it will cost you plenty."

"Sure, sure."

"It will cost you one hundred thousand?"

"What?"

"To be donated to the Milk Fund. The show is on tonight, and the sale of tickets was poor. Depression, you know."

Partages stuck out his pudgy hand. "Okay, Eddie boy. Go to

it. Only"—he held on to Ed's hand—"be careful. I'd rather have you alive than the money."

"I'll be careful, Mr. Partages," Ed told him grimly. He watched the theater owner get into a taxi headed for home; then he flagged one himself, said curtly, "Giuseppe's Restaurant!"

GIUSEPPE VERDADI PETRONESCA weighed two hundred and ten pounds. His round Venetian face, adorned with an immense walrus moustache, beamed good nature and convivial hospitality at Ed as the latter entered his restaurant.

"Gooda even', Mister Race! You no come here longa time. You gonna have dinner now? We gotta swell chicken dinner for a dollar and a half—an' you getta bottle of wine free. No cheap belly wash, but real Chianti!"

Ed said, "Hello, Giuseppe!" He looked around the restaurant at the dozen or so people who were eating.

Giuseppe had run a speakeasy here throughout prohibition, and now he operated a nice high-class restaurant, with a public dining room on the main floor and private rooms upstairs for parties and affairs.

Ed took Giuseppe by the arm, led him toward the rear, where a small door opened to the staircase. "Look, Giuseppe, I'm sure your chicken and Chianti are swell. But I didn't come to eat tonight. I have to see Manny Sloss and Joe Ricci. What room are they in?"

The proprietor stopped short in front of the door, faced Ed desperately. "Mister Race, you no go upstairs. I no want no fights in my place. Those guys gotta party upstairs, and they no want to be disturb'."

"I suppose they've been up there all evening?" Ed asked. "You didn't see them come down, did you?"

Giuseppe shrugged, his face blank. "I no see nothing, Mister Race."

Ed said softly, "Get out of the way, Giuseppe."

The fat man stared at Ed for a minute, and then lowered his gaze before the cold look in Ed's determined eyes.

Ed added, "It'll be better for you if I go up; it may save you a raid by the police. And I'll do my best to avoid a fight—though I can't promise anything."

The proprietor moved reluctantly aside. "They in room four, Mister Race." He put his hand on Ed's arm. "You try for make me no trouble?"

Ed nodded, stepped through the doorway, and mounted the flight of stairs. Room four was down the corridor, and he could hear sounds of merriment and laughter from behind the closed door.

He tapped on it softly, and the noise died within. A voice said gruffly, "Well, come on in!"

Ed turned the knob, stepped into the room.

Six people were seated around the table, eating. Beside the table was an iced wagon with champagne bottles, and there were three empty bottles on the floor.

Three of the six were girls, pretty, all blondes, lavishly lipsticked and painted, and all slightly gay. Manny Sloss and Joe Ricci each sat beside a girl, and the third man, who, Ed guessed, had driven the sedan in which they had left Slingel's office, had his head on the table. The girl next to him was trying to pour champagne down the back of his neck.

Sloss and Ricci tensed when they saw who it was and started to push their chairs back. Sloss exclaimed: "Hell! I thought you was the waiter!"

Ed grinned at them, said, "Don't be alarmed, gentlemen. I just want to talk to you."

Ricci asked, "About what?"

"About a lot of money in a Boston bag."

Ricci and Sloss glanced at each other. Sloss pushed his chair back and stood up. "We don't know what you're talking about, Race."

"Naturally," Ed told him, "you wouldn't. You've been here all evening, I suppose."

Ricci nodded quickly. "That's right. We're celebrating Mona's birthday." He indicated the blonde who sat next to him.

"So you wouldn't know," Ed went on, "that Slingel and Partages were held up and robbed of about a half a million dollars between them."

"You don't say!" they both exclaimed in unison.

"And now, gentlemen, I'd like to talk a little business with you"—and as they started to refuse, Ed added—"before the police get here."

Ricci glanced at Sloss, who pondered for a moment, then nodded. Ricci looked at the girls. "Scram!" he ordered.

Mona and the one who sat next to Sloss arose reluctantly. The one who was pouring champagne down the drunken man's neck looked up and protested shrilly: "Say, I ain't going to leave Mickey like this. Let me wake him up with champagne first!"

Ricci just looked at her fishily, repeated, "Scram!"

At the look in Ricci's eyes, she quickly put down the glass, arose and joined the other girls. When they had left, Ed said genially, "Now, gentlemen, I know just how bad you feel. You haven't got your guns with you because you parked them with the Boston bag. You wanted to be clean when you were picked up by the police."

He saw the faces of both of them turn a pasty green.

"But don't worry. I'm not going to hurt you."

RICCI SAID hoarsely, "All right, Race, we know you seen us coming out of Slingel's. But it's no good. Your word against the three girls', and Giuseppe and the waiters. They'll all swear we were here all the time."

Ed nodded. He said, as if talking to himself: "A man could go far with a quarter of a million dollars."

Sloss took a step nearer.

"What's the meaning of that crack?"

Ed smiled at him. "Here's a proposition, Manny. You give me back the money you took from Partages, and you can keep what you took from Slingel. I understand there was more in his safe than what Partages had."

Sloss frowned. "You're nuts, Race. If we did that, the country wouldn't be safe for us. You know how much drag Slingel's got. He'd bury us in the can for life!"

"I understand," said Ed. "But—suppose Slingel was dead!"

Both Ricci and Sloss gasped. "Dead!" Sloss exclaimed. "Boy,

what a break that would be. We'd be left with the dough, and nobody to turn it over to!" A slow smile spread over his face, only to disappear immediately. "But—who?"

"Suppose," Ed said slowly, "I were to tell you that he's dead?"

Sloss and Ricci stared at him as if he were a ghost.

"You mean," Ricci demanded, "that you knocked him off in the office?"

Ed grinned. "If you'd just bumped somebody, would you go around talking about it? I'm not saying what happened. Mind you, I'm not saying I did anything at all. But if he *were* dead— how about my proposition? I'd see to it that Mr. Partages made no complaint about the robbery. You could go wherever you liked, and I'd forget about the whole thing."

Sloss asked eagerly: "Well, is he dead?"

"I don't know—yet," Ed said doubtfully. "Let me use the 'phone."

He stepped over to the corner where the instrument sat on a small end table, picked it up and gave the number of the State Emergency Hospital on Eighty-fifth Street.

Mickey was still dead to the world, with his head on the table, but Sloss and Ricci hung breathless on his every word.

When he got the hospital he asked for the emergency ward, then asked to talk to Nurse Sweeney.

"Hello, Elaine," he said. "This is your old friend, General Sherman."

"Well, if it isn't Eddie Race!" Elaine Sweeney exclaimed. "Imagine hearing from you! I thought you'd forgotten I was alive. What's new with you, Eddie? I saw your act at the Partages

Theater last week, and it was a wow. The old eye is as good as ever. I was boasting to the girls about how you used to take me out—"

"Listen, Elaine," Ed interrupted, glancing at Sloss and Ricci out of the corner of his eye, how's that bird that was brought in to the hospital from Forty-ninth Street a little while ago?"

"Who, the one with the broken jaw? That was a nasty crack he got. You know him?"

"No, but I did it to him. Will he die?"

"Die? Of course not. Why should he die? It'll take a few weeks—"

"You don't say so!" Ed exclaimed. "He died ten minutes after he was brought in, eh? Too bad, too bad. Keep it quiet about my phoning, will you, Elaine? Well, goodbye."

Puzzled, Elaine demanded: "What's the matter with you, Eddie? Who said he died? What are you talking about? I said he'd be better—"

"Yes, sure," Ed interrupted. "I didn't think he'd live. Did he talk before he kicked off?"

MISS SWEENEY'S voice grew more and more exasperated. "Are you crazy, Eddie? Nobody died here today. I didn't say anybody died. Listen, Eddie, I hate to think it, but are you phoning from the nuthouse? You certainly—"

"He didn't talk at all?" Ed went on imperturbably, nodding violently to Sloss and Ricci. "Well, I didn't think he would. I'm surprised he lived that long."

He hung up on Elaine Sweeney's maddened voice: "Eddie, if you don't talk sense I'm going to hang up on you!"

He looked at Sloss and Ricci, and they stared back at him silently.

Finally Ricci said almost under his breath, "You—bumped—Slingel!" There was awe and admiration in his voice.

"I didn't say anything of the kind!" Ed Race said wrathfully. "What do you want me to do—sign a confession?"

"No, no," Ricci protested placatingly. "You don't have to admit anything. We'll keep it under our hats. No one'll ever get a peep outta us."

"All right," Ed said, mollified. "But get this—I never said anything about bumping Slingel. If you boys want to draw your own conclusions, okay."

"That's okay!" Sloss said hastily. "It's okay by us, Race!"

"All right, then. What about Partages' money?"

Sloss and Ricci were both laboring under great excitement.

"Sure, sure. You can have it back. We got plenty from Slingel—enough to take us to the coast. Come on—we'll take you where we cached it and give you Partages' share."

They lifted Mickey between them, helped him through the door, which Ed held open for them. Sloss explained:

"We can't leave him. He'd talk too much. Besides, there's plenty for the three of us."

Ed stopped them. "Just a minute, boys," he said tightly. "I hope you haven't got any ideas of crossing me on Partages' money. Because if you have—" He looked at them significantly.

"Don't worry," Sloss assured him. "You can come right with us and collect. We got the bag checked in the Grand Central

Station. We were supposed to meet Slingel there at eight o'clock. Instead, we'll take a train for the coast."

They half-carried, half-dragged Mickey down the stairs. In the restaurant, the three girls were sitting at one of the tables. Mona came over.

"Well," she said, "I hope you're through with the heavy conference."

"Listen, kid," Sloss told her, "we got something big on. We'll be out of town for a week, maybe, and then we'll wire you dough and tell you where to come. Now, beat it, quick, the three of you."

Giuseppe stared unbelievingly at the sight of Sloss and Ricci coming out in such friendly fashion with Ed Race, but he said nothing, watched them leave with a puzzled expression.

Outside they hailed a cab, and Sloss said, "Grand Central, buddy—Vanderbilt Avenue-side."

Ed sat on one of the extension seats, and Sloss and Ricci put Mickey between them on the rear seat.

At the station, they left Mickey in the cab, went in with Ed and got the bag from the check room, returned to the cab. They told the driver to go and get himself a sandwich, then they opened the bag. It was crammed with bills of large denomination—none less than a thousand.

Ricci watched greedily while Sloss counted out two hundred and fifty thousand, handed the bulky wad to Ed, who distributed it in all his pockets.

Ed said, "Okay, boys. Don't bother to count the rest. It's yours."

"Listen, Race," Sloss said. "We're takin' your word that we don't get picked up before we leave town."

"You have my word," Ed assured him, "that Partages will make no complaint to the police. You won't be picked up on his account. I can't answer for how you make out with Slingel."

Ricci grinned. "You took care of him."

"What do you mean?" Ed demanded sharply. "Did I say anything about taking care of Slingel?"

Ricci continued to grin. "Sure not, Race, sure not! You never even seen him in your life. That's okay with us."

"As long as you understand that," Ed told them coldly.

He got out of the cab as the driver returned, watched them drive into the ramp of the Grand Central Terminal. There was a train leaving for the coast in twenty minutes, and he was sure they'd be on it.

He walked to the corner, went into the 'phone booth in Liggett's Drug Store, and 'phoned Partages.

"Listen, Eddie boy," the theater owner bubbled excitedly, before Ed had a chance to say anything, "come up here quick. Don't waste a minute. Slingel is here. And boy, will you be surprised!"

"What's the trouble?" Ed asked.

"Trouble? Plenty of trouble. Get down here quick!"

Ed hung up, went outside and got another cab up to Park Avenue and Sixtieth, where Partages' penthouse apartment was located.

The Jap servant let him in, conducted him to the library,

where Partages was pacing up and down, his fat face bathed in sweat, while Slingel fidgeted on the edge of his chair.

Ed looked from one to the other. "You both look as if your wives have presented you with sextuplets," he commented. "What are you all stewed up about?"

Slingel smiled sourly, glanced at Partages. "You tell him, Leon."

Partages came over to Ed, grabbed the lapel of his coat. "Did you hear what happened?"

"You've got me all agog," Ed told him. "Hurry up and spill it before I have a nervous breakdown."

Partages fairly shrieked at him: "*Gray Mama* was disqualified after the race! She *didn't win!*"

"What!" Ed turned to Slingel for confirmation.

The bookie nodded. "You don't have to take my word for it, either. There's Leon's newspaper on the table."

"The whole story is in there," Partages hurried on. "They found out that *Gray Mama* was doped up, and they disqualified her. Payment on all bets is held up. Only for Slingel being so anxious to pay me off, I wouldn't have got the money at all!"

"So what?" Ed asked, looking at Slingel.

SLINGEL SHRUGGED. "Well, Leon has to give me back the two hundred and fifty thousand. I paid it to him in good faith. But since he was robbed, I'm willing to take a licking; I've taken plenty of them in the past. He can give me fifty thousand, and I'll give him back his receipt and call it square."

"I won't do it," Partages said stubbornly. "I was robbed in your office. You should have given me some protection—"

71

He stopped and stared at Ed. For Ed Race had begun to laugh—loud and uproariously.

Slingel stood up, frowning. "Don't be a clown, Race. There's nothing funny—"

"Wait a minute—" Ed stopped him. "Maybe I can straighten this out. Let me talk to Mr. Partages in private for a minute, and maybe I can convince him that he ought to accept your proposition."

Slingel said incredulously: "You want him to do it?"

"Sure. You lost plenty on the deal, didn't you?"

Slingel regarded him suspiciously for a moment, then shrugged. "I didn't think you'd be for me, Race. I sure appreciate it."

He stepped to the door. "I'll wait in the foyer. Call me when you're ready."

When he had gone, Partages said resentfully, "Look here, Eddie boy, I'd of thought you'd be the last to want me to pay that skunk. I'm convinced now that the robbery was a frame-up—"

While he was talking, Ed was pulling money from his pockets, dumping it on the table. He counted out a hundred and fifty thousand, put the rest back in his pockets.

Partages gasped. "Where did you get it?" He clutched Ed's sleeve. "Eddie boy! You—got that money back for me!"

"There's a hundred and fifty thousand. One hundred thousand goes to the Milk Fund. You can give Slingel fifty thousand and still have a hundred grand left. Slingel expects to meet his boys at eight o'clock and get his money back. He has a surprise coming to him."

Partages scooped up the money, counted out fifty one-thou-sand-dollar bills, put the rest in the drawer of his desk. Then he waited until he had a straight face and went to the door. He called Slingel in.

"If it wasn't for Eddie Race," he told the bookie, trying to keep a serious expression, "I wouldn't do this. Here's fifty thousand."

Slingel brightened. He counted the money, put it away, and took from his wallet the receipt for the money, handed it to Partages, who tore it to bits.

"Well," said the bookie, "I'm taking an awful baking on this."

Ed grinned. "You don't look so sorry." He took Slingel by the arm, escorted him to the door, watched him until the elevator came up and the gate opened. Just as the gate was closing, he called after him: "Say, Slingel. If you see Sloss and Ricci, give them my regards!"

The gate closed on Slingel's startled face, and Ed came back into the library, chuckling.

He waved Partages aside, reached for the telephone, and called the State Emergency Hospital.

"Listen, Elaine, this is your nutty boyfriend. Don't get sore. I was just pulling a fast one on a couple of friends before. Can I make it up to you?"

"How?" she asked coldly.

"I'll take you to the Milk Fund Benefit tonight. There'll be big doings. I'm appearing, and also there'll be an anonymous contribution made, of a hundred thousand dollars. How about it, honey?"

"Okay, Eddie, I'll go, if you'll promise to act saner than you did on the 'phone before. Honest, I thought you were cuckoo. By the way, who's nutty enough to contribute a hundred thousand dollars to the Milk Fund in a lump like that? It wouldn't be you, would it?"

Ed chuckled, winked at Partages, who was watching him and grinning like a cat.

"Keep it to yourself, Elaine. The anonymous contributor is none other than Nick Slingel—only he doesn't know it yet!"

MURDER BACKSTAGE

E D RACE said: "Listen, miss, if that gun is loaded, please turn it the other way!"

She was only a slip of a girl, barely more than nineteen, and she was dressed in a trim-fitting gray, tailored suit with the jacket cut low to reveal the white skin of her throat. Her little breasts were rising and falling spasmodically, and her dark eyes flashed with panicky nervousness that was borne out further by the way the hand which held the automatic shook.

She had come into Ed's room at the Longmont without knocking, leaving the door an inch or two ajar, and had caught Ed in his shirtsleeves in the act of tying his cravat before the dresser mirror. Ed's coat was in the closet, together with the two heavy forty-fives in shoulder holsters. The four other revolvers that he used in his act at the Clyde Theatre were in the little black bag on the dresser, almost at his elbow, but they might as well have been a mile away for all the good they did him.

The girl said in a tight, strained voice: "Raise your hands—keep them in the air."

Ed let go of the ends of his cravat, and half-turned to face her. He could hardly believe that she meant business. "What is this—a holdup?" he asked her. In spite of the menace of the automatic, his eyes ran appreciatively over her slim figure. "I have to admit, you make a swell-looking lady bandit."

The girl stared at him intently, breathing hard. "You're Ed Race, The Masked Marksman, aren't you?" she demanded almost in a whisper. "The one who does the gun-juggling act at the Clyde Theatre, and shoots out the candles on the stage?"

Ed nodded, half-smiling. "That's the name, miss. Now, what's the game?"

She didn't answer, but raised her voice slightly, called out: "It's all right. You can come in."

The door behind her was pushed further open, and three men entered. They were strangers to Ed. The first was a stout man with a genial face and small eyes. He wore a purple-checked vest under a tan single-breasted suit, and his paunch stood out so far

76

that the ends of the purple vest flapped when he walked. The other two men were tall, thin, and both had the pinched features and bright pinpoint eyes of confirmed dope addicts. One wore a peaked cap and the other a black derby hat. They both had automatics in their hands, though the fat man appeared to be unarmed.

The one in the derby came in last, closed the door behind him and double-locked the catch.

The girl moved to one side, still keeping her gun trained on Ed. She said to the fat man: "Well, I did it for you. I hope you're satisfied."

The fat man beamed at her. "You have done excellently, Sylvie, my dear. I'm sure Mr. Race would never have permitted a mere male to get the—ah—drop on him the way you did." He patted her on the shoulder, glanced at his two companions, noted that they had their guns trained on Ed. "You may give me your gun now, my dear. Your work has been exceedingly well done. You shall have the—ah—paper in the morning."

She released the gun to him. "B-but you said you'd bring it along with you."

"So I did, my dear, so I did. And I always keep my word." He took a small folded slip of green paper from his right-hand vest pocket. It looked to Ed Race like a folded check. "Here it is, my dear. You see, I brought it."

THE GIRL extended her hand for it, her thin little face shining eagerly. But the stout man smiled unctuously, drew it away from her grasping fingers, and put it back in his vest pocket.

"Not quite yet, my dear, if you don't mind. First let us get this

business satisfactorily completed, and you shall have your paper."
He led her courteously to a chair, gently propelled her into it.
"Just sit here quietly, Sylvie, until we are through with Mr. Race."

Ed, who had been standing with his back to the dresser,
scowling at the two gunmen, now glared across at the girl, said
bitingly: "So you can't even get paid off. You ought to know
better than to expect a square deal when you do the dirty work
for three cheap palookas that haven't got guts of their own—"

The two gunmen snarled, and the one in the peaked cap took
a step forward. "Listen, you!" he rapped. "Button up that lip, or
I'll bust in your face—"

The fat man stopped him. "Tut, tut, White, my boy. You
should control yourself. Such language!" He sighed, rolled his
eyes, then said to Ed: "You must excuse my friend, here. He is
not accustomed to conducting business deals in a quiet manner."

Ed exclaimed: "You birds must be crazy. This is a hotel room.
All I have to do is raise my voice—"

The fat man looked shocked. "My dear Mr. Race! That would
be equivalent to suicide! You must understand, sir, that I am
familiar with the construction of this hotel. It is a modern structure, planned for the comfort of the guests. It is entirely sound-
proof; even the doors, as you see, are lined with sound-insulating
material. And what is more, Mr. Race, these pistols of ours are
only twenty-two caliber weapons—quite capable of piercing a
man's brain at close range, but making very little noise."

Ed glanced at the girl, who was sitting wide-eyed, with her
hands clenched in her lap. Her lower lip was quivering; she had

lost the self-possession of a few moments ago. Ed said resignedly to the fat man:

"All right, Napoleon, I admit you're a brainy guy. Now what's the gag?"

The gunman in the peaked cap moved impatiently, growled: "Let's lay off the comedy. We ain't got all night!"

The stout man nodded agreement. "Quite so, White, my boy, quite so. Still, I wish you would let me do things in my own way. Your methods are so—ah—crude."

The gunman grumbled: "Aw, why all the talk—?"

"Yes?" The fat man almost hissed the word. Suddenly his face seemed to have lost all its good nature as he stared at the pinch-faced one in the peaked cap. Just the one word he said, but the gunman's face became a pasty yellow, and he cringed before the basilisk stare in the fat man's eyes.

"I—I didn't mean nothin', boss. Whatever you do is okay by me."

The fat man turned away from him without another word, and spoke to Ed smoothly, as if nothing had happened:

"Now, if you will permit, Mr. Race, I will make introductions. I am Mr. Brown; this—ah—gentleman in the cap, who appears so eager for action, is Mr. White; and this—" indicating the one in the derby hat—"is Mr. Black."

He beamed at Ed as if he had said something extremely clever. "Brown, White and Black. Those, believe it or not, are our names!"

"And mine," Ed told him sourly, "is Green. Now that we all

know each other, suppose you tell me what nuthouse you all escaped from."

Mr. Brown's genial fat face wreathed into a deprecating smile. "You should be more careful of your language, Mr. Race. For myself—" he shrugged "— I am old and tough-skinned; I can stand insults. But my friends, Mr. White and Mr. Black, are quite different. As you may have noticed, they are very high-strung individuals—"

"You mean they're cokeys!" Ed interrupted. "Come on, let's get this farce over with. What do you want here?"

MR. BROWN became crisp, businesslike. "We are here to make you a proposition, Mr. Race. We hope you will accept it, as we would rather not use force—" He extracted a wallet from his coat pocket, took out a sheaf of money, and placed it on the dresser beside Ed, then stepped back quickly.

Ed picked up the money, riffled through it. He raised his eyebrows as he noted that there were no bills less than fifties or hundreds.

Mr. Brown went on: "There is five thousand dollars, Mr. Race."

Ed started to laugh. "You certainly went to great lengths to give me this money, Mr. Brown. First you send this girl in, then you bring two hoods along—where's the catch?"

"The catch, Mr. Race, is that we are going to ask you to do something for that money."

"Naturally."

"You are billed to appear at the Clyde Theatre tonight. Your number is timed for 10:35—" He consulted a heavy gold watch that was strung on a gold chain which spanned his capacious vest. "— exactly one hour from now. What we want you to do is this: my friend Mr. Black, here—" He nodded toward the derby-clad gunman, who smiled broadly, showing a double row of false teeth. "— is also an expert marksman and juggler. He is not quite as good as you are, Mr. Race, but he'll do. Well, in short, we want you to let him take your place at the Clyde tonight!"

Ed said: "Sorry, Mr. Brown, or whatever your name is. Your proposition smells bad. No business." He extended the sheaf of money toward the fat man. "You can have this back."

Mr. Brown did not take the money. He made a peculiar, clucking sound with his tongue and his upper palate, and looked sorrowfully at the two gunmen.

"What do you think of that, boys?" he asked. "He won't do it!"

"To hell with him!" snarled Mr. White. "Let's knock him off and get going."

Mr. Brown seemed to be considering the suggestion. "I'm afraid that's what we'll have to do, White, my boy." He shook his head reprovingly at Ed, and his double chin waggled back and forth. "You shouldn't be so obstinate, Mr. Race."

The girl had been listening tensely all this while, picking nervously at invisible threads in her skirt. Now she sprang up from her chair.

"B-but," she cried, "you p-promised me Mr. Race wouldn't be hurt. You c-can't kill him!"

Mr. Black pushed his derby hat back on his forehead, placed a hand on the girl's shoulder. "Sit down, twist!" he barked. "Or get knocked down!"

Ed's eyes blazed. For some reason he felt that the girl, in spite of what she had done, needed protection. "Leave her alone," he said coldly.

Mr. Brown exclaimed hastily: "Yes, yes, Black, my boy, leave her alone. Just keep Mr. Race covered, the two of you, while I make the necessary arrangements." He stepped over to the telephone beside the bed. "Er—ah—do not hesitate to shoot him, boys, if he should make the least suspicious move. He is an extremely dangerous man."

Ed was standing with his back to the dresser, and he saw the murderous gleam in the eyes of both gunmen. Coked up as they were, they might even shoot without any provocation at all. Ed calculated the distance to the door, but gave up the idea for two reasons—first, because those two automatics would have belched lead at him the first step he took; second, because even if he succeeded in getting outside the room, he feared what the two gunmen might do to the girl.

He stood tense, still clutching the sheaf of money, while Mr. Brown plumped his weight down on the bed, picked up the telephone and glibly gave the number of the Clyde Theatre. It occurred to Ed that whatever it was that these men had in mind, they must have planned it very carefully indeed, to have noted the number of the theatre, and to have checked the time when the Masked Marksman act was scheduled to go on.

EVERYBODY IN the room was tense while Mr. Brown waited for his connection. The two gunmen had now turned their attention entirely to Ed, and they were keeping their pistols beaded on his stomach. The girl had produced a tiny handkerchief from some mysterious recess about her person, and she was twisting it in her lap while she bit her lip. Her eyes were on Ed, and they seemed to be trying to convey some sort of message to him.

Suddenly Mr. Brown said into the transmitter: "Hello, hello, is this the Clyde Theatre? I want to talk to Mr. Forbes, the manager." He was a marvelous actor, for his voice changed as he spoke, became crisp and professional in tone.

"This is Doctor Brown, Mr. Forbes—Doctor—ah—Winfield Brown. I—ah—am calling you in behalf of one of your actors—a Mr. Edward Race. I regret to inform you that Mr. Race has been suddenly taken ill at his hotel—touch of tonsillitis, you know— and I fear he must remain in bed. What's that? No, no, it will not be necessary, sir. I have already invited a consulting specialist."

Mr. Brown winked broadly at Ed and the two gunmen, went on talking into the 'phone. "Mr. Race has asked me to inform you that he is sending down a very good friend of his by the name of—ah—William Black, who is an expert marksman and juggler, and who will take his place. Mr. Race says that he is certain his friend will make out all right, and it will not even be necessary to announce the change, since he always appears with a mask anyway. I beg your pardon, sir? Yes, Mr. Black is leaving now, and will be there in ample time. He is bringing along an assistant. If you will give your doorman instructions to admit them both—thank you, sir. I will give Mr. Race your regards, and inform him of your best wishes for his speedy recovery.... No, I think it best that nobody from the theatre visit him until tomorrow.... Goodbye, sir."

Mr. Brown hung up, and beamed at Ed. "You perceive, Mr. Race, that we really didn't need your cooperation."

Ed glanced at the two gunmen, frowned. "I don't get this yet. Why go to all this trouble to have Blackie here impersonate me?"

Mr. Brown didn't answer. He had suddenly become a dynamo of energy. He took the small black bag off the dresser, opened it, exclaimed: "Ah—four revolvers! The others must be with your coat." He went to the closet, came back with Ed's other two forty-fives and exhibited them to the man in the derby hat, who took one, hefted it in his free hand, and nodded approval.

"What do you say, Black, my boy?" Mr. Brown asked him. "You should be able to do your work well with these, eh?"

Mr. Black said: "Yeh!" and continued to concentrate his attention on Ed, while the fat man put all six revolvers back in the bag, took from his pocket a small mask, and dropped that into the bag, too.

"You see, Mr. Race," he said, "we have provided for everything. And now we are ready. White, my boy—" He put his pudgy hand on the shoulder of the one in the peaked cap. "— it will be your duty to keep Mr. Race and this young lady—ah—amused until we 'phone you that our work is finished. If you can avoid—ah—killing them, why, so much the better! However—" he paused significantly "— use your own best judgment."

Ed Race said nothing, while Brown and the man in the derby backed out of the room, Brown carrying the small bag.

When the door had closed behind them, Peaked-cap locked it. Then he straddled a chair backward, facing Ed and the girl.

He rested the barrel of the automatic across the back of the chair, and grinned nastily.

"Sit down, Race," he said. "You got a while to wait."

Ed asked him: "What are you birds up to—are you figuring on robbing the Clyde Theatre?"

Peaked-cap continued to grin. "Pretty smart for a dumb actor. You're guessin' fine!"

The girl uttered a little gasp. "B-but Mr. Brown told me it was only to win a bet. He said he had made a large bet that his friend could impersonate the Masked Marksman, and he stood to win a lot of money, so if you wouldn't agree, they would just tie you up for a while—"

ED LAUGHED harshly. "He stands to *make* a lot of money. The take at the Clyde is about sixty thousand dollars. The treasurer brings the money backstage to the office at ten-thirty every night, and this fellow will be there with my guns—"

"That's right, pal," Peaked-cap broke in. "An' my friend, Mr. Black, will just give him one slug through the head—another for the guard—an' he's off with the dough. No stranger could ever get backstage. But they'll never be lookin' for a holdup from the guy that's doin' the Masked Marksman number!"

Ed glanced sideways at the girl. She was moaning softly to herself. "I—I never knew it was anything like this. I—I would never have—"

"Why did you do it, miss?" Ed asked her gently. "How did they make you do it?"

"I—I did it for Jerry," she sobbed. "Jerry forged a check to make good a shortage at the theatre, and Mr. Brown got hold of the check. He said he'd give it back to me if I did this for him."

"Jerry?" Ed asked, frowning. "Who's Jerry?" He glanced at the gunman, who was evidently enjoying the whole thing very much from behind the muzzle of his automatic.

Suddenly Ed's eyes narrowed. "You mean Jerry Forbes, the treasurer of the Clyde—John Forbes' son?"

She nodded miserably. "Jerry and I are engaged. I happened to overhear a conversation in Jerry's office and learned about the check. Mr. Brown was trying to get Jerry to do something or other, and Jerry wouldn't do it. So when Mr. Brown left, I went after him, and when Mr. Brown found out who I was he told me all about it, and said I could get the check back if I did something for him."

Peaked-cap said gleefully: "Ain't it a scream, Race? Jerry Forbes wouldn't frame a holdup with the boss; he says he'd rather take the rap for the forged check. So what does this dame do, but practically walk up to the boss and hand him the lay on a silver platter!"

Suddenly the girl uttered a choked scream.

Peaked-cap frowned at her. "Do that once more an' you get a slug, see?"

"I don't care," she sobbed. "Kill me, kill me! I don't want to live. They'll kill Jerry now, and I'm the cause of it!"

Ed could see that she had been too stunned up to this moment to realize the peril that threatened Jerry Forbes. He felt genuinely sorry for her. He knew Jerry by sight, had heard a good deal about the lad from John Forbes, the grizzled old general manager of the Clyde Theatre.

Old Forbes had had a good deal of trouble with Jerry. The boy had quit college in his sophomore year because of some sort of scandal that his father had hushed up; then he had gotten into one scrape after another, until John Forbes had given him a job at the Clyde. Young Jerry seemed to have settled down at last, and sufficiently won the confidence of his father to have been appointed treasurer of the theater.

Ed had heard of Jerry's engagement to a girl named Sylvie Sumter, but he had not at first connected the name.

Peaked-cap chuckled wickedly. "You ain't heard the richest part of it, Race: that there check that she's beefin' about—Jerry Forbes made it good. He come clean with his old man, got the dough, an' brought it over to the boss. But the boss kept the check. An' the dame, here, didn't know Jerry made it good."

Ed said softly: "I get it. Brown is never going to give that check back. If he or his pal, Blackie, kill Jerry tonight, it won't matter. But if they pull off the robbery without murder, they'll hold the check over Jerry's head to make him keep quiet!"

Peaked-cap nodded, his bright little eyes glinting madly. "That's the stunt, pal. An' you, being a close friend of old John Forbes, won't let out a peep neither. Smart, huh?"

The girl half rose from her chair. "You fiend!" she shrieked. Her voice rose high, hysterical. "You've tricked me—"

The gunman got up, kicked his chair away. His eyes were mere pinpoints now, his lips twisted into a murderous snarl. With the generous dose of the drug that Mr. Brown must have given him, he was capable of anything now. "I told you you'd get it if you yelled, didn't I? Well, here it is." He thrust the automatic out toward her.

ED'S JAW bunched in rage, and he tensed his muscles for a leap at the other. But the gunman didn't fire, for abruptly the jarring jangle of the telephone cut into the tenseness of the moment.

Ed pulled up short as he saw the tautness of the gunman's hand relax. Peaked-cap exclaimed: "Gawd! They done the job already!" He backed toward the telephone, swinging his gun so as to keep Ed covered. The girl slumped in her chair in a faint.

Ed glanced at his wristwatch—it was only 10:05; too early for the holdup to have taken place—the money was never moved until 10:30. It must be somebody else.

Peaked-cap kept his eyes on Ed as he lifted the receiver, said eagerly: "Yes?"

Ed saw the gunman's face drop, and heard a familiar crackling into the receiver. It was Halloran, the house detective of the Longmont, who habitually talked with a foghorn voice. Ed could hear him distinctly from where he stood:

"Hello, is Mr. Race sick or something? The telephone operator tells me there's a doctor up there that called the theater to say he wouldn't be there."

Peaked-cap kept his beady eyes on Ed, rested the automatic on the end table upon which the telephone stood. Ed Race could barely restrain a grin. He had always known that the inquisitive telephone girl at the switchboard listened in on calls, but this was the first time he didn't mind.

Peaked-cap said: "That's right. He ain't feeling well. He don't want to be annoyed, so better not come up. Now hang up an' don't bother us."

He slammed the receiver down on the hook, glared at Ed. "If anybody knocks at that door, you tell him to go away, get me? Try to start anything, an' I'll let you both have it."

Ed Race said: "That was Halloran, the house detective. He's no fool. He'll guess something is wrong up here. Better get out while you can."

"An' leave you so's you can 'phone the Clyde? Nix. If anybody breaks in on us, it'll be just too bad."

Ed shrugged. "The girl's fainted," he said. "Let me get her some water."

"Stay right where you are!" the gunman snarled. His eyes flicked to the slumped-over, pitiful figure on the chair. "I ought to give it to you both, an' scram. If the boss had listened to me—"

Ed Race suddenly became aware that he was still holding on to the sheaf of money that Mr. Brown had given him. He glanced at his wristwatch again. 10:16—only fourteen minutes before the holdup would take place. Jerry Forbes would die; perhaps others. Desperately he sought a way out. He'd have to take long chances now. Even if Halloran came up, it was doubtful whether the gunman would hesitate to shoot, coked up as he was.

Ed held out the sheaf of money. "Am I supposed to keep this?" he asked.

"Like hell!" Peaked-cap exclaimed. "Give it here!" He held out his left hand, came closer.

Ed veiled his eyes to hide the elation in them. He feigned reluctance. "Didn't Mr. Brown say I was to have it?"

"Never mind what Mr. Brown said. I ain't passin' up five grand. Give it here, I say!"

Ed sighed, said: "Well, take it." He extended it awkwardly, and let a few of the bills dribble out of his fingers, flutter to the floor. Peaked-cap's eyes followed them instinctively. It is not in human nature to disregard fifty and hundred dollar bills floating through the air. Ed's psychology was excellent.

IN THE moment that the gunman's eyes were off him, he acted with all the synchronized speed that his years of acrobatic juggling on the stage had developed in him. His left hand darted out swiftly and surely, gripped Peaked-cap's gun hand and twisted it mercilessly. Ed's fingers were like iron bands.

The gunman's face went ashen under the punishment. He uttered a hoarse cry of rage, clawed at Ed's eyes with the dirty nails of his left hand. The automatic exploded into the floor, then fell from his numbed fingers. Ed's bunched fist came up like a rocket, caught him over the temple with a sickening thud. Peaked-cap's mouth fell open, and he buckled over, sank to the floor. He lay still in a crumpled heap. Ed didn't know whether or not the blow had killed him, and he didn't care.

He sprang to the side of the girl, who had slid from the chair to the floor. He raised her head and shook her violently. There was no time now for coddling. His wristwatch read 10:19—only eleven minutes left.

Someone rapped at the door, and Ed called out: "Who's there?"

"It's me—Halloran. What's goin' on in there? I thought you was sick."

Ed left the girl, who hadn't revived under his shaking, and unlatched the door. Halloran came in, stared at the gunman and the girl on the floor, grinned at Ed:

"What the hell—who's loony now? This is a respectable hotel, Race—"

Ed wasn't paying any attention. He was across at the telephone, jiggling the hook and keeping his eye on the watch. "Get police headquarters," he fairly shouted into the instrument. "Quick—it's life or death!"

The operator downstairs said: "Oh, hello, Mr. Race! I thought you were sick. Mr. Halloran just went up to see you. How do you feel?"

Ed gritted his teeth. It was 10:20. "Listen, Nora," he yelled, "get police headquarters, did you hear? A man is going to be shot in ten minutes, *Get busy!*"

"Oh," said Nora. "Why didn't you say so?"

She kept the line open, and Ed heard her asking for headquarters. He held the French 'phone, and watched Halloran, who had gotten some water from the bathroom for the girl. Halloran was dipping his fingertips in the glass and flicking the water in her face.

"What's on the ball, Race?" he asked. "Why all the commotion? Who's the palooka on the floor?"

Ed told him tersely: "He's one of a gang. They're going to hold up the Clyde Theatre in ten minutes, posing as me—"

91

Halloran whistled, and Ed swung back to the instrument as he heard the voice of the headquarters operator. He said:

"Get a radio car over to the Clyde Theatre on Forty-ninth Street. It's going to be held up at ten-thirty. The treasurer, backstage. Two men—"

The operator said: "Wait a minute. I'll give you the radio room."

Ed stewed another half-minute, while the girl opened her eyes under Halloran's treatment, then got the radio room and started to tell his story over again.

The sergeant at the other end exclaimed: "Say, listen, if you're pulling something, you'll get in plenty Dutch.

You want us to send a couple men to barge in on the Clyde, an' grab the Masked Marksman? You're nuts. We know the Masked Marksman—he's—"

"I tell you," Ed broke in frantically, "*I'm* the Masked Marksman. I'm Ed Race. This man is impersonating me—"

"And I'm the king of China," the sergeant jeered. "Where you calling from?"

"The Longmont Hotel."

"Then hang up and we'll call you back. We're not sending a radio car without knowing who sent us—"

Ed banged the instrument down in disgust. He was sweating under his collar, and his hands were clammy.

"It's no good, Halloran," he said bitterly. "Let's go. We've got to do this ourselves."

"Do what?"

92

"Never mind. Come on. We're going around the corner to the Clyde, and we're going fast. I'll tell you on the way."

THE GIRL, who had just come to, watched them go out, her mouth open, still too dazed to recall the situation. As they got out into the hall they heard the telephone back in the room ringing.

"That's headquarters," Ed said bitterly. "They'll get around to it—after it's all over!"

"You can't blame 'em," Halloran told him. "You sound screwy to me, too!"

Down in the lobby, Nora, the switchboard operator, caught a glimpse of both men making tracks for the street, and startled the one or two guests who were about by shouting across to them:

"Mr. Race! Police headquarters is calling. They—"

"Connect them with my room," Ed called to her. "There's someone there."

He had Halloran by the arm, and was rushing him out before the startled operator could frame another question. In the street, pedestrians stared at them, got quickly out of their way. Ed was still holding the automatic.

Over on Broadway, Halloran exclaimed breathlessly: "Ye gods, Race, the hotel will fire me, and chuck you out. Ever since you've been staying here the place is like a madhouse. The boss was just bawling me out—"

Ed's watch showed 10:26 as they swung around the corner. The lights on the marquee of the Clyde Theatre halfway up the block showed them a black sedan at the curb, facing west, away from them. A man in a gray topcoat was pacing back and forth beside it, smoking.

He saw them running, got a glimpse of Ed's face under a streetlight, saw the automatic, and his hand streaked.

Ed didn't stop running, but his automatic barked sharply, flamed, and the man staggered, clawed the air and fell against the sedan, sank to the pavement.

"That must have been their lookout," Ed panted. He clutched Halloran by the arm, swung him into the alley that led to the stage entrance. The doorman saw him coming, exclaimed:

"Hello, Mr. Race, we thought—"

He stopped, gulped, and ducked aside as he saw Ed's gun, saw the service revolver Halloran had drawn. Inside, Ed and Halloran raced down the narrow entryway; Ed, who was in the lead, barged into a property man whom he sent sprawling, and swung into the wide space backstage. Several of the actors standing in the wings turned to stare at them.

He noticed the figure of Mr. Black, wearing the little mask of the Masked Marksman, standing close beside a large packing case, holding two of the big forty-five caliber revolvers, and watching the iron staircase across the other end of the house, which Jerry Forbes would descend when he came from the box office.

And close to the foot of that staircase, in an attitude of great unconcern, stood Mr. Brown.

Mr. Brown saw Ed, but Mr. Black did not. Mr. Black was too busy watching that staircase.

At the moment that Mr. Brown saw Ed, Jerry Forbes appeared

at the head of the stairs, carrying a gray, canvas money-bag that was stuffed to capacity. Just behind him was the armed guard who always accompanied him.

Ed caught the plan at once. The staircase had no railing on one side—was little more than an iron ladder. Mr. Black would fire just two shots, one for Jerry Forbes, one for the guard. Jerry would be hit, would drop the canvas sack at the feet of Mr. Brown. Before anybody could realize what had happened they would both be outside, in their car.

And that was just what was happening. Mr. Black had raised one of the revolvers, was resting it on his left forearm to steady his aim; he was drawing a bead on Jerry.

WHEN MR. BROWN saw Ed, his hand came out of his coat pocket, with a gun. The whole thing happened so fast that the telling of it can give no adequate impression of the suddenness with which Ed Race was presented with the necessity of making a decision. It was evident that Mr. Black and Mr. Brown would fire at the same time—the one at Jerry Forbes, the other at Ed.

So that if Ed shot the fat Mr. Brown, Jerry Forbes would die; but if Ed shot Mr. Black, it would be equivalent to giving up his own life for Jerry.

Sometimes, in a critical situation, a thousand thoughts, a thousand pictures will flash through a man's mind in the space of a split second, with kaleidoscopic rapidity. Into the mind of Ed Race there came only one picture—that of Sylvie Sumter, sitting tense in the chair back at the Longmont and crying: "I don't want to live!" when she realized she had sent young Jerry Forbes to his death.

And Ed Race fired at Mr. Black....

The slug caught Mr. Black in the side of the throat, before he could squeeze the trigger of the revolver he was holding.

Ed didn't wait to see the effect of his shot—he *knew* it had gone where he wanted it to; in eight years of vaudeville training he had never missed a shot on the stage. Even as the wicked bark of the fat Mr. Brown's gun seemed to echo Ed's shot, Ed went into a running somersault *toward the stout man!*

He had done the same thing often on the stage, had even shot out the flame of a candle across the stage upon coming out of the somersault. Now he heard the whine of the bullet, felt the *thudding* impact of it against his right shoulder.

He landed on his feet, still rushing toward Mr. Brown, whose face had lost all its pleasant geniality. Mr. Brown was trying to get another shot at him, but Ed's movements made him a difficult target.

From behind Ed, Halloran's service revolver roared thunderously. But Halloran missed—the slug clanged against the iron staircase beside which Brown was standing. Above him, Jerry Forbes and the guard had stopped short. Jerry clutched his canvas bag, while the guard fumbled with his own gun.

Brown's gun barked again, but Ed Race had dropped to the floor, rolled on his unwounded shoulder while he transferred the automatic from the right hand to the left. And then, before the fat man could find his target again, Ed, from the floor, squeezed hard on the automatic, let it pump its seven remaining slugs into Brown's body.

Out front, on the stage, the performance continued as usual; John Forbes, the manager of the theater, had appeared in the wings and was frantically signaling the Peterman Brothers to prolong their xylophone act.

And behind the scenes, Ed climbed to his feet on the arm of Halloran, while the actors, property men, electricians, crowded around them asking a hundred questions. Jerry Forbes and his guard raced down the iron staircase, stepped over Mr. Brown, and hurried to Ed's side.

"You've saved my life, Mr. Race! I saw you shoot that man!"

Jerry's father, John Forbes, pushed his way through the crowd. "Are you hurt badly, Ed?" he asked. "I've sent around the corner for Doctor Gray. He'll be here any minute."

Ed demurred, "Only a flesh wound."

FOR A moment his eyes met those of the grizzled old manager, and there was a suspicion of tears in John Forbes' eyes. He put his arm around his son, still looking at Ed Race. "I—I can't say what I feel, Ed," he husked.

"Never mind," Ed said, as the sound of a police siren came to them from outside. "I have to do something."

He pushed Halloran away, walked a little unsteadily, with blood flecking the right sleeve of his coat, over to the body of Mr. Brown. Kneeling beside him, he turned the body over, inserted his fingers in the fat man's vest pocket, drew them out with a green slip of check-paper.

He glanced somberly toward the doorway, and his fingers

worked swiftly, tearing the check into small bits while the two uniformed policemen who had come in began to question the actors.

John Forbes exclaimed: "We'll have to get another number to substitute for the Masked Marksman. Who's ready?"

Ed called out to him: "Get my guns together—I'm going on myself as soon as I get my shoulder bandaged. Here comes the doctor now." He said to the little, bustling, bespectacled Doctor Gray, who had come straight over to him: "Get your things ready, Doc; I'll be right with you."

Ed pushed his way through the excited crowd, took young Jerry Forbes by the elbow and led him to one side. He pressed the scraps of torn paper into the young man's hand. Jerry Forbes stared at the pieces for a moment, then a glad light showed in his eyes. "You—you got the check back, Mr. Race!"

Ed said: "In a little while I guess Sylvie Sumter will be here. Tell her—this is a wedding present to you and her from—the Masked Marksman!"

DEATH'S UNDERSTUDY

THE FRANTIC telegram Ed Race, the Masked Marksman, received from Art Jennings was typical of the ex-bootleg baron:

ED RACE,
C/O PARTAGES VAUDEVILLE CIRCUIT,
NEW YORK, N.Y.

    REMEMBER ART JENNINGS DID A BIG FAVOR FOR YOU IN TULSA, OKLAHOMA QUESTION MARK YOU SAID YOU WOULD DO THE SAME FOR ME SOMETIME STOP WELL THE TIME HAS COME STOP YOU ARE THE FAIR-HAIRED BOY TO DRAG ME OUT OF A TOUGH JAM STOP I AM ON THE UP AND UP IN HARMONVILLE BUT IF YOU DO NOT FRONT FOR ME I WILL BE DEAD BY MONDAY NIGHT STOP I SEE BY PAPERS YOU PLAY HARMON-VILLE STARTING MONDAY STOP WELL IF YOU WANT TO SEE ART JENNINGS ALIVE AND KICK-ING YOU BETTER COME RIGHT OUT TO SEE ME WHEN YOU HIT TOWN STOP MY ADDRESS IS FIVE-TWO-FOUR PERRY STREET STOP SO LONG SEE YOU SOON.

ART JENNINGS

Ed Race had the telegram in his pocket when he got off the train at Harmonville Monday afternoon. He saw that his baggage was unloaded and properly marked for delivery to the Harmonville Theater. The only piece of luggage that he took with him was the small black bag that contained the four heavy forty-five caliber revolvers, similar to the two which hung in the twin holsters under his armpits.

These were the guns that he used in his juggling-and-target act, and he always carried them with him. He didn't look upon them as ordinary revolvers; he had used them every day now, for eight years, and in addition to being the means by which he made his living on the stage, they had often brought him safely out of many tight spots where the unerring response of those perfectly calibrated guns to the pressure of his trigger fingers had meant the difference between life and death.

Ed Race was the "Masked Marksman" of vaudeville fame; the man who was billed throughout the country on the Partages and affiliated circuits as: "The Man Who Can Make Guns Talk." But besides that, his insatiable craving for excitement and danger had led him into the hobby of crime detection—he held licenses to operate as a private detective in a dozen states—and many people had availed themselves of his services in the past, always without charge, just as Art Jennings was doing now.

Ed Race felt a pleasurable tingle as he strode through the station to the street. The prospect of action always raised his spirits. At the Union News Stand he bought a copy of the *Harmonville Evening Star* and glanced at the headlines. He had learned that the quickest way to acquaint oneself with conditions in a

new town was to consult the local papers. This one certainly gave him an eyeful. The headline was smeared black across the page:

VIGILANTES STRIKE AGAIN!

The four-column spread at the left threw further light on the telegram in Ed's pocket:

Glenn Bowen, General Manager of Jennings Gas Stations is Shot in Broad Daylight by Black-Hooded Leader of Vigilantes!
The mysterious body of men who call themselves "The Vigilantes" are continuing their reign of terror by adding murder to their previous atrocities. The Jennings chain of gas stations

101

seems to have become the butt of their hatred. After bombing one gas station yesterday....

ED RACE ceased reading, folded the paper and made his way out of the station. He had read enough to realize how badly Art Jennings needed him.

He got into a sedan that stood at the curb with a "For Hire" sign on the windshield and asked the driver: "How far out is 524 Perry Street?"

"About a mile and a half," the surly driver shot back. "Just outside the town."

"Let's go," Ed said. He looked out the cab window at the busy town as the driver tooled the car out of the traffic around the station, swung left into a side street. They were proceeding north, but Ed noted that they were apparently avoiding the main streets. He swung his gaze forward, past the driver's shoulder, and his eyes narrowed.

Something had seemed to be lacking, and he discovered suddenly what it was. Every public motor vehicle, he knew, was required by law to carry liability insurance, and to paste a sticker in the windshield as evidence that the insurance had been paid for the current month. There was no such sticker in the windshield of this car; moreover, Ed noted that the driver had removed the "For Hire" sign.

Ed said nothing, but he watched carefully the direction in which they were going. He saw that they were proceeding along a back street that ran parallel to the main thoroughfare of the town. By glancing down the side streets that they passed, he could catch an occasional glimpse of the traffic on the main street, only a block away.

Looking down one of these side streets, he caught sight of a large theater structure, saw the big sign which announced:

HARMONVILLE THEATER
Beginning Today—
THE MASKED MARKSMAN

A few blocks further on, he saw that the driver was watching him in the rear-vision mirror, and he sat back in his seat, feigning weariness by half closing his eyes. The driver stepped on the accelerator, and the car spurted forward, slowed down again once it had passed the next intersection. Ed Race's mouth tightened in a grim line. He guessed why the driver had sped past that particular corner; for his keen eyes had caught what the driver had apparently wanted him to miss—the signpost of the intersection. The name of the cross street they had just left behind was Perry Street. Ed was not being taken to the address he had given.

Soon the buildings began to thin out, until they were in a semi-country section. The streets were not graded here, and there were only one or two houses on a block.

They passed a gas station with a sign reading:

JENNINGS SERVICE STATION
Tank Up With
GOOD GAS!

The street they were traveling along merged with another,

became a paved road. Here there was another gas station, with the same sign. Ed recalled what he had heard about Art Jennings—that the retired bootlegger had moved out here, invested his money in a chain of gas stations, and that he was doing as well legitimately as he had done during prohibition.

Suddenly the driver slowed up, swung off the concrete into a dirt road, and ground along in second up a short hill. He pulled up before a frame building that was almost surrounded by tall, majestic evergreen trees. The house gave evidence of having once been the home of a wealthy person, but it was now in disrepair. The paint was gone in many spots, the walls and gable roof were weather-worn, and the grounds in front were overgrown with weeds. There was no sign of life....

Ed had moved forward in the car to one of the collapsible seats, and had put the black bag on the floor beside him. He was close to the driver's compartment now, and he said, "This isn't Perry Street, is it?"

The driver turned slowly. He was grinning and licking a small split in his lower lip.

"Maybe this *ain't* Perry Street, guy," he announced. "But it's where you're going—like it or not!"

At the same time, his hand came up over the partition, into view. It held a blunt-nosed automatic that was pointing at Ed. "See what I mean, guy?"

ED NODDED. "I get you." He lowered his eyes so that the other should not see his purpose. And he moved so swiftly that it was impossible to tell which of the several things he did occurred first. Daily practice on the stage—with sensitive, hair-triggered revolvers, where the deviation of a sixteenth of an inch in aim or movement might mean the failure of his act—had developed in Ed Race a supreme coördination of mind and muscle and eye which resulted in lightning-quick action.

It is certain that the driver did not see Ed's left hand sweep up until it had struck the wrist that held the automatic; nor could he possibly have followed with his eyes the blinding swiftness with which Ed's right hand traveled to and from his left armpit holster to emerge with the big forty-five that descended in a short, vicious arc to crack against the luckless driver's forehead.

The automatic exploded once harmlessly into the cushioned seat of the car, as the driver's hand tightened on it convulsively. Then he dropped it from nerveless fingers, sagged across the seat, unconscious. A thin rivulet of blood trickled from his forehead under the peaked cap, where Ed had hit him with the barrel of the revolver.

Ed's eyes were bleak, cold. He glanced swiftly toward the house, to see if anyone had taken notice of the single shot. No one appeared. He left the driver lying inert across the front seat, got out of the car and approached the house, revolver still in his hand. He didn't draw the one in the other holster because he was carrying the black bag in his left hand. The afternoon was dying, and there were shadows around the front door of the house.

Anyone but Ed Race would have gone away from there as quickly as possible. But not Ed. He had to find out what made things tick—why the driver had brought him here; what, if anything, was inside that house.

Suddenly he stopped short, tensed. A wisp of smoke was

coming from the stone chimney at the north end of the house. Someone was in there, making a fire in the fireplace.

Almost at the same instant, the front door slid open a couple of inches, and the short, ugly barrel of a sawed-off shotgun yawned out at him. Ed was less than thirty feet from the doorway, and he knew what a sawed-off shotgun could do to you at that distance.

A hard voice from inside called out sharply, "You're covered, Race. Drop that gun and come inside. Don't start anything, and you won't be killed."

Ed stood taut for a moment, trying to gauge the location of the voice. If it were directly behind the door, a slug from his forty-five might reach the owner....

He gave up the idea as he saw a shadow moving behind the open window to the right of the door.

The same voice from the doorway hurried on, as if hoping to sell him an idea: "There's three of us here, Race. We're sure to get you, if you start shooting."

Ed said, "All right, you win." He bent slowly, placed the revolver on the ground. "It has a hair trigger," he explained. "If I drop it it'll go off."

The voice said, with a note of relief: "Okay, okay! Snap it up!"

Ed stood erect once more, having left the revolver at his feet. He was still holding the black bag. In the act of bending, the fingers of his left hand had worked swiftly with the catch, and now the bag was unlocked, ready to sag open the moment he released his hold on it.

He advanced slowly toward the house, noting that a second

shotgun had appeared at the open window. They weren't taking any chances on him.

The door opened, revealing a darkened hallway. A grayish figure stood, half-screened by the door, holding the shotgun. Beyond, a dull glow came from a room at the left.

Ed stepped in, and the door was immediately slammed shut. A flashlight glared in his face, and the same voice directed him: "Go down the hall, and into that room, Race." The edge of nervousness was gone now; the speaker probably felt that he and his men had the upper hand.

Ed said nothing, turned and obeyed. He heard the footsteps of the one man behind him, heard him joined in a moment by another—probably the one who had been at the window.

HE REACHED the room from which the glow was coming, stepped inside, and stared. A man in a black hood and a flowing white garment of some sort of cloth was kneeling before the fireplace, stirring a black, thick liquid in an ordinary scrubbing pail. The pail was resting on a couple of logs that had just begun to burn.

The man in the black hood glanced up from his task, and Ed saw that the hood was slitted for eyes and mouth. The gown had a large red letter "V" embroidered in the center, over the man's chest.

Ed smiled grimly and said, "So you're the Vigilantes, eh?"

The man at the fireplace didn't answer. He turned back silently to his task of stirring the black liquid. Ed glanced across the room, saw what made his blood boil: a newspaper was spread upon the floor, and on it was a pile of chicken feathers.

The two men with the shotguns had come in, leaving the door open, and they were staring at him, not saying anything, letting the situation sink in. Ed noted that their hoods, unlike that of the man at the fireplace, were white instead of black. Finally, the one who had done the talking before said, "You get the idea, Race?"

Ed's right fist clenched at his side. He glared into the two masked faces, from which two pair of eyes peered at him through narrow, slitted holes.

"Yes," he said hotly. "I get the idea. You're three yellow-bellies that haven't got the courage to stand up and face a man—so you cover yourselves up and hide behind masks. I bet the three of you haven't got a nickel's worth of guts between you!"

For a moment, he thought that those two shotguns were going to spit death at him. The hands of the two men clenched on the stocks of the guns, and the nearest took an involuntary step forward. But the one behind him exclaimed: "Take it easy, brother. We'll have him talkin' a different tune before we're through with him. Let's tell him the story, an' then go to work."

The other nodded his hooded head. "Race," he said, "we brought you out here just to give you a little talking to, a kind of warning to leave town. But after what you did to our man outside, we're going to tar and feather you and ride you out of town. But just in case that don't teach you a lesson, I'm telling you that if you come back here, we'll kill you. Understand— we'll kill you!"

Ed bit back his anger. He wanted to find out what he could from these men. He wanted to keep them talking as long as possible, so he could observe them, notice any little things about them that would enable him to identify them later. For instance, he saw that the spokesman, the one nearest him, had a hangnail on the third finger of his right hand. If he didn't bite or cut it off, Ed would remember it when he saw him again.

He kept his eyes on them, studying their build, the way they stood, the size of their shoes. While he studied them he said, "Do you mind telling me what you have against me? To my knowledge, I don't know a soul in this town. Why—?"

"You lie!" the man with the hangnail snarled. "You're a friend of Art Jennings. He sent you a telegram to come here. Well, we don't want men like Art Jennings in this town. We've given him forty-eight hours' notice to sell out and get out, and believe me, if he isn't out by midnight, he won't get off as easy as you!"

"I see," Ed said softly, fingering the bag.

"And what's more," the other went on, "you should be thankful that we're only giving you a dose of tar and feathers instead of a dose of lead!" He turned his head slightly toward the black-hooded man at the fireplace, said almost deferentially, "What do you say, chief? Can we get started?"

The man at the fireplace looked at the pitch, got to his feet and lifted up the pail from the fireplace with a piece of cloth which he wrapped around the handle. He still said nothing— Ed thought bitterly that he was smarter than the others, for no one would be able to identify his voice later—but he nodded as if in a signal to the man with the hangnail, who jerked his gun at Ed, demanded: "Will you take your clothes off yourself, or will we do it for you?"

ED SAID meekly, "Wait a minute, will you?" He transferred the black bag from his left hand to his right, under the watchful eyes of both white-hooded Vigilantes. The man with the black hood had carried the pail to the other side of the room, near the window, and was spreading the feathers out flat on the newspaper.

Suddenly, as if by accident, Ed's black bag came open, and the chamois-covered revolvers tumbled out to the floor. The eyes of both Vigilantes followed the contents automatically; and in that second, Ed's left hand flashed in and out of his right armpit holster. He pivoted so that he was sideways to them, and the heavy forty-five filled the room with the thunderous reverberation of its roar.

The two Vigilantes were hurled backward against the door as if a typhoon had struck them. They never had a chance to fire their shotguns. Ed fired twice, for the heart each time, and he never even bothered to watch for the effects of his shots. He knew those two men would be dead before they hit the floor.

He pivoted to the left on the heel of his left foot and the toe of his right, so that his gun swung in line with the third man at the other side of the room. But the third man didn't like the idea apparently, for he thrust his hands in the air and stood still, not saying a word.

Ed said, "All right, brother, take that hood off and let's see your face."

Brother started to obey reluctantly, but before he had got the string untied that held the hood in place, there came the sound of the front door banging open, and of footsteps rushing down the hall.

Ed glanced toward the doorway, saw the driver of the car—the one he had hit—appear there, flushed, bloody-faced, holding the big revolver that Ed had left on the ground outside. He was snarling, as his glance traveled from the two dead bodies on the floor in hood and gown to the tall, poised figure of Ed Race.

He swung up the big forty-five, fired at the same moment that Ed did. But the driver was not accustomed to the hair-trigger on that gun. His finger tautened on it a split second too soon, and the revolver exploded before it was quite in line with Ed's chest; the slug tore into the fireplace at Ed's left, without touching him.

Ed Race's bullet caught the driver between the eyes. His body went hurtling back into the hallway, crashed to the floor there, to the accompaniment of the thunderous echoes of the shots.

The little room was filled with smoke and noise and the stench of pitch and powder as Ed swung toward the man in the black hood. That gentleman had decided that this was no place for him. He had been standing close to the window, and now Ed caught a blur of motion, heard a smashing of glass—the hooded man had leaped head first through the closed window.

Ed saw his feet go sailing out, got a flash of brown shoes disappearing, but held his fire. He could easily have hit him, but he couldn't bring himself to shoot at an unarmed, fleeing man—even though that man had planned to tar-and-feather him.

The man had kicked over the pail of pitch in his haste, and it was oozing out over the floor. Ed ran around it, peered out into the dusk. The hooded man disappeared around the corner of the house just as Ed stuck his head out of the window. In a moment, there came the sound of a starting motor from the rear, and a car flashed out along the gravel path, careened crazily past the sedan out front, and skidded into the road, shrieking down the hill and out of sight.

Ed watched it go, smiling grimly. He could have stopped that car with a single well-placed shot at the rear tire. But he let it go. Three men dead was enough of a day's work, considering that he had been in town for less than half an hour. And he could get this one whenever he wanted to; for he had noticed something that would inevitably identify the fugitive—the hooded man had stepped in and spilled pitch as he leaped for the window, and there, plainly outlined, was the mark of a rubber heel. And there were seven little round marks in a semicircle in that heel print—the marks made by the seven small suction cups.

Ed let the car go and stooped closer to examine the print. He noted that the mark left by the third suction cup from the right was not as distinct as the others; it must have been clogged with mud or dirt. He picked up a sheet of newspaper and laid it over the print, so that it would not be disturbed by anyone who might enter; then he stepped gingerly among the bodies of the three Vigilantes, recovering his revolvers.

He put the four chamois-covered ones back in the black bag, reloaded his other two, and replaced them in their holsters. He left the bodies just as they were and went out of the house; got into the sedan and turned on the ignition key, which the driver had left there.

Slowly he drove back in the direction of the town....

NUMBER FIVE-TWENTY-FOUR Perry Street was a two-story frame, typical of a town like Harmonville. At one time, not so long ago, it had probably been surrounded by half a dozen acres of cultivated ground from which the owner had managed to raise a living. Now, however, the town had grown up around it, the business section had encroached further and further north, until the cultivated land had given way to graded streets and rows of stores.

Five-twenty-four sat about twenty feet back from the street, with another twenty feet of lawn on either side of it and a garage in the rear. Along the street on both sides were rows of stores, and cars were parked vertically at the curb. It was right around the corner from Main Street, and two blocks down was the Harmonville Theater, where Ed was booked to open that evening.

As he parked the borrowed sedan in front of Art Jennings' house, it occurred to Ed that he hadn't even notified the manager of the theater of his arrival. That would have to wait, however, until he saw Jennings.

At Ed's ring the door was not answered at once, but a small wicket which must have been especially built into the door slid open, and a face appeared—one that Ed knew. It was Lee Krane, one of the special bodyguards that Art Jennings used to take around with him wherever he went, in the old days.

Ed said, "Hello, Lee. How've you been these five years? Never mind the passwords; just let me in quick."

Lee Krane grinned through the wicket, even as he unlatched the door. "The boss will sure be glad to see you, Race. He was beginning to think you was giving him the go-by, like all the other muggs that used to 'hello' him when he was a big shot."

"I wish I had," Ed said ruefully, as he stepped in and followed Krane upstairs. "Jennings seems to be in plenty of hot water in this town."

Krane put away the heavy automatic he had been holding and clumped up the stairs. "Okay, Jake," he called up. "Tell the boss it's Mr. Race."

The room they entered fronted on the street and was equipped as an office. Near the window, Art Jennings sat at a desk littered with papers. He was about forty, bald, short and stocky. He had grown much stouter since Ed had seen him last, and he was no longer the domineering, tough genius who had built up a million-dollar-a-year bootleg organization during prohibition. Rather, he was the epitome of the small-town businessman.

Ed could hardly restrain a grin at seeing him there. He nodded to Jake, another bodyguard, who was leaning against the wall, blowing smoke rings, then he stepped over and shook hands with Jennings.

Jennings seemed nervous, fidgety. He said, "You're a white guy, Ed, to come to the front for me. Not many would do it."

Lee Krane sauntered over to the desk, chewing on a tooth-pick. "Well, boss," he said, "if Mr. Race don't pull us out of this jam, we might as well pack up and scram."

Jennings frowned. "Scram nothing! I never ran from anybody yet, and I ain't running from a pack of yellow Vigilantes." He got up and came around the desk. "You ought to meet these guys, Ed. They're—"

"I've met them already, thanks," Ed told him dryly. "Four of them, in an old house just outside the town. I got into a taxi at the station that must have been planted there for me, and the driver took me out there."

"Hell," exclaimed Krane. "That's why I missed you at the station. I just come back from there, thinkin' you hadn't got in yet. That's why the boss was feelin' so bad."

Jennings broke in impatiently: "What happened, Ed? How'd you get away from them?"

"I didn't. They got away from me—that is, one of them did. The other three won't ever try to tar-and-feather anybody again."

"You mean you croaked them?"

Ed nodded.

Jake, the other bodyguard, threw away his cigarette and came over. "No kidding, Mr. Race—did you smoke three of them guys just now?"

"No kidding," Ed told him. "At least, I don't think they were kidding. They looked pretty dead to me."

Lee Krane groaned. "Boy, those birds won't wait any twenty-four hours anymore. They'll gang up on us now. We're as good as cooked!"

JENNINGS GLARED at Krane, said to Ed, "A fine bunch of rods I got here. Since we went legitimate, they've got soft. They get the heebie-jeebies if anybody gives them a dirty look!"

Krane shuffled, lowered his eyes, and looked at the floor. "Aw, Gee, boss, we can't fight the whole town—"

"Listen," Ed broke in, "I'm in a hurry. I haven't reported at the theater yet. There are three dead men out at that house, and

I'll have plenty of explaining to do when the cops find them. They'll probably turn out to be prominent citizens of the town. So suppose you give me the lowdown on what's been happening here, and why they suddenly decided they didn't want you after you've been here three years."

Art Jennings was standing close to Ed, and he had to look up to talk to him. He said savagely, "I'll tell you why they don't want me. I'm a legitimate guy, Ed. I wasn't a dope. When prohibition went by the board, I quit, paid my income tax to the government, and came out here. I had a half a million bucks cold cash, and I invested it right in this neighborhood. I built gas stations. I've got fifteen of them in a radius of thirty miles, and each one cost twenty grand to build. Everything is on the up and up. My nose is clean with the government, see? I just take these two palookas"—he gestured toward Jake and Lee—"along with me for old times' sake.

"Well, what happens?" He poked his finger in Ed's face. "I ask you—what happens?"

"I give up," Ed said. "What happens?"

"Some wise guys start eyeing my string of gas stations and try to figure a way to take 'em away from me. They form these Vigilantes and suddenly decide I ain't a model citizen. They send me this!"

He snatched up a pencil-scrawled slip of paper from his desk, thrust it at Ed. "Read it! Imagine trying to scare me—Art Jennings—with stuff like that!"

Ed took the note, scanned it:

Jennings:

This is a clean town. We don't want carrion like you. We don't want you living in this town, or doing business in this town. You have twenty-four hours to sell out and get out. A word to the wise is sufficient!

The Vigilantes

Ed finished reading, looked at Jennings and grinned. "So they couldn't scare you, Art? Only you sent me a telegram that sounded like you were green in the gills!"

Jennings shook his head. "It wasn't the note that scared me, Ed. I took the note to Captain Smiley at headquarters. He said he'd investigate, but it would be pretty hopeless to find out who the Vigilantes were. All right. I sat tight. So yesterday they bombed one of my stations, and they knocked off Bowen. Bowen was my best man—worth both of these. I would almost have stacked him up against you. Well, they knocked him off."

Jake spat and said, "The dirty so-and-so's! They shot him in the back!"

Jennings went on. "Well, it began to look like we didn't have a chance. How could we protect fifteen gas stations? So I went down to old man Drayton at the bank and asked him could he get me a buyer. Sure, he could get me a buyer—" Jennings spat out the words—"fifty grand he could get me, for a chain of stations that cost close to half a million! Do you get the idea, Ed? They're riding me!"

Ed's eyes wore a faraway expression. "Did you say the name of the man at the bank was Drayton? What's his first name?"

"John Drayton," Jennings told him. "His son—say!" He

snapped his fingers suddenly. "I never thought of that—his son is Paul Drayton, the manager of the Harmonville Theater!"

"And did Drayton tell you the name of the customer he could get who was willing to pay you the fifty thousand?"

"No. But he said he had a letter from a lawyer in New York, authorizing him to offer that amount." Jennings' eyes were shining eagerly. "You see, Ed, it all looks like a plan to freeze me out of here."

Lee Krane broke in, saying, "Listen, boss, what're we going to do now? Those vigilante birds will be out to get square for the three guys Mr. Race bumped off—"

ED STOPPED him impatiently. "Quit the croaking, Lee. The worst that can happen to you is to get killed." He went on, addressing Jennings. "I still don't see why you had to get panicky and wire me. The police ought to be able to give you plenty of protection." He sighed wearily. "But now I'm in it. I suppose the Vigilantes won't give me any peace, either." He picked up his black bag, started for the door.

"Where you going?" Jennings asked anxiously.

"Over to the theater," Ed told him. "I'll report to Drayton and see what I can find out from him about his old man. You stick close to the house here, and don't let anyone in."

Jennings came after him, held on to his sleeve. "Look, Ed, I'm worried about you. You're lightning with guns, but you can't stop a bullet in the back. Let me send one of these palookas with you. They're not much good, but they'll do in a pinch."

Ed hesitated, studied Jake and Lee somberly. "All right," he said suddenly. "I'll take Lee Krane, and leave Jake with you. I might need somebody to back up my play."

Lee Krane said, "If you think I'm yellow, Mr. Race, you just wait and see. I'll blast the guts outta them Vigilantes!"

They left Jennings and Jake upstairs, made their way outside to the street.

Ed said, "We'll walk to the theater. The police may have the number of that sedan."

Ed kept his eyes peeled on the way down Main Street. Krane walked beside him with his hand in his jacket pocket all the time. But no one molested them.

At the theater, Krane glanced up at the electric light sign in the marquee which read:

Tonight—The Masked Marksman
Special Engagement for One Week

He said, admiringly, "You got what it takes, Mr. Race. There ain't anybody I know could shoot out them candles on the stage the way you do. How's it feel to be a vaudeville star?"

Ed grunted. "Damned inconvenient—when your friends keep getting you in trouble." He led the way around the corner to the stage entrance, nodded to the doorman.

"I'm Ed Race," he said, showing his identification card for the Partages Circuit.

The doorman glanced at the card, looked queerly at Ed. "Mr. Drayton didn't think you'd show up," he told Ed. "You better go right up to the office and see him. I think he wants to talk to you."

119

Ed shrugged and went through, with Krane at his heels. He crossed backstage, nodding to several actors whom he knew, who were already there for rehearsal. Many of these people he hadn't seen for years. The Harmonville Theater was part of a second-class chain, and Ed had never played here before. He had been switched to this booking because the business of the theater had fallen off considerably in the last few months, and the canny Leon Partages had thought that a star act like Ed's might revive it.

The manager's office was upstairs on the balcony floor. Ed gave the black bag to Lee Krane and said, "Wait for me out here. I want to talk to Drayton in private." He knocked at the door and entered without waiting.

Drayton was a small man, with spare, mouselike hair and weak blue eyes. He was in the act of getting up from his desk when Ed stepped in and said, "I'm Race. You wanted to see me?"

Drayton stared at him, blinking for a moment, then said haltingly, "Glad to know you, Mr. Race. I've heard a lot about you."

Ed waited, silent, studying him.

Drayton fidgeted, picked up a paper from the desk. "About your billing here, Mr. Race—I—er—" He hesitated, then rushed on: "I'm having your engagement canceled. You can't appear!"

Ed frowned, came closer to the desk. "Why not?" he rapped.

For answer, Drayton gave him the paper he had taken from the desk. "I—I got this a little while ago. It was left at the box office by a messenger boy."

ED TOOK the paper, stared at it. It was written in the same kind of pencil scrawl as the note that Jennings had:

120

Paul Drayton:

We don't like to hurt you because you've lived in this town a long time. But you better do what we tell you. Ed Race, the one who does the Masked Marksman act, is billed to appear this week. Well, we don't want him. You cancel his act and send him back where he came from. If you don't you'll have plenty of trouble—Race won't live till morning, and you won't have any theater left to run.

The Vigilantes.

Ed gave the letter back to Drayton. "Who are the Vigilantes?" he drawled.

Drayton looked scared. "I swear I don't know, Race. Their leader never says a word—he lets the others do the talking. He wears a black hood instead of a white one like the others. He fired the shot that killed Bowen. Nobody knows whether his neighbor is a Vigilante or not."

Ed looked thoughtful. "I think," he said slowly, "that I'll be able to lay my hands on that black-hooded leader. He got away from me once, but he left something behind."

Drayton asked eagerly, "What—" He stopped as a knock sounded.

Ed swung around, facing the door, his right hand caressing the knot of his tie, where it was not far from his shoulder holster. "Come in," he called.

The door opened, and a stocky man in a dark blue suit entered. He stared sharply at Ed from under his bushy gray brows, then demanded of Drayton: "Who's this?"

Drayton gulped, said, "Captain Smiley—this is Ed Race."

121

Ed looked past the accompanying detective sergeant, saw Lee Krane outside the open door, peering in. He called out, "Come on in, Lee. I might be a while—it looks like a conference."

The detective sergeant barred the doorway, glanced for instruction to Captain Smiley. The captain frowned, but nodded, and the sergeant stood aside for Krane to enter, then closed the door behind him and stationed himself with his back to it.

Lee Krane shuffled from one foot to the other in the presence of the police captain, and glanced suspiciously at Drayton.

Captain Smiley turned to Ed. "You killed three men a little while ago."

Drayton uttered a startled gasp, swung wide-eyed to look at Ed. "My God, Race! You shot the Vigilantes?"

Ed paid no attention to him, but asked Smiley, "How did you hear so quick?"

"Somebody 'phoned headquarters and reported it. I've just come from there."

Ed said coldly, "They were Vigilantes. They kidnapped me, had tar and feathers ready. They were all armed. The police department of Harmonville wasn't doing me any good, so I had to defend—"

SMILEY RAISED his hand. "Just a minute, Race—don't get the wrong idea. I'm not arresting you, or asking for an explanation. You see, we've checked the fingerprints of those three men, and it looks as if the federal government owes you a vote of thanks—as well as a little reward. Those three yeggs belonged to the Costello gang, which the police of a dozen states have been hunting—the ones that kidnapped August Lemmerer in nineteen-thirty-three!"

Drayton exclaimed: "Then—then they're not—Harmonville men? They—"

"They weren't real Vigilantes," Ed told him. "They were imported gunmen, who were brought here for the sole purpose of driving Art Jennings to sell his gas-station holdings."

Smiley nodded in agreement. "That's how we figure it. But we don't know who their leader is—the one who wears the black hood. He's the boy that we'd like to lay our hands on. With him still at large, Art Jennings will never be safe. It's easy to get more gunmen—"

"How about working from the New York end?" Ed asked him. "The lawyer who made the offer to Drayton's father at the bank—"

"We've already asked New York to check on that. It's a blank wall. The lawyer refuses to talk; he says his client's name is confidential. But we've got something else to work on."

Drayton took an involuntary step forward as Smiley went on: "The leader of these so-called Vigilantes checked his hood and gown in a parcel in one of the automatic lockers at the railroad station. But he was careless. He must have slammed the door of the locker and gone away without making sure it was locked. The station attendant noticed it, and took the parcel out. We have a standing rule here that whenever a locker is opened the contents must be examined by the police. Sometimes stolen goods are left in them."

Ed exclaimed, "And that parcel contained the hood and cloak?"

Smiley nodded. "If we should get our hands on the leader, the thing that would convict him would be the key to that locker. He'd probably have it still."

"Another thing that will convict him," Ed said, "is his heel mark. He left the mark of his heel in the pitch out there, in that house where they took me. He got away while I was shooting it out with the others. It was probably he that 'phoned you, thinking I'd be held for a while."

"I saw that," Smiley said, "and had it photographed. It might have been yours."

"All right," Ed told him. "Take a look." He half-turned, raised first one heel, then the other."

"That settles it," Captain Smiley said.

"Now," Ed went on, "I suggest you take a look at the heels of everybody that might have an interest in buying out Art Jennings. You might start with us."

Drayton flushed. "Just because my dad had that offer from the lawyer—"

"If you're not the man we want," Ed said coldly, "you won't mind showing us."

"All right," Drayton yielded. "If it'll give you any satisfaction—" He turned and lifted his feet as Ed had done a moment ago. His heels did not have suction caps. They were flat, worn down.

Ed said, "I didn't expect that your heels would match that print. Your shoes are black; the hooded man's were brown."

"He might have changed his shoes," Captain Smiley said doubtfully.

"I didn't!" Drayton protested. "And if you want to search me for that locker key, you can do that, too!"

Ed put a hand on his shoulder. "It's all right, Drayton. I'm sure you're not the man. The leader of those Vigilantes is someone who has New York connections, who could recruit gunmen."

His eyes rested speculatively on Lee Krane. "How about you, Lee? You know a lot of rodmen. You might have been the one to plan a thing like this."

LEE KRANE grinned. "You can take a look at my shoes any time, Mr. Race." He turned around, raised his heel slowly. But he did not complete the movement. Suddenly he seemed to stumble, recovered his balance, and came erect facing them, snarling viciously, with the blunt-nosed automatic in his hand.

Drayton uttered a gasp of dismay, cowered back from the murderous gleam in Krane's eyes. Captain Smiley and the sergeant were caught cold.

Ed Race, however, had plunged into action almost at the moment that Krane swung around. He plunged to the floor on his hands and knees, then sank prone, rolled over once and struck Krane's legs.

Krane, who had not entirely recovered his balance after swinging around, went staggering backward against the wall. He lowered the muzzle of his automatic to fire into Ed Race's body on the floor at his feet. But Ed's revolver was already out of its holster, and its deep-toned roar filled the room, echoing outside through the theater. The shot traveled upward, tore through the top of Krane's head.

Ed rolled free of Krane's falling body, got to his feet and stared at the others.

Smiley exclaimed: "God! That was quick. I've never seen a man move so fast in my life!"

Ed said, "If you had to practice twice a day on the stage, you'd be fast, too." He pointed down at the twisted, gory body of Krane. "There's your Vigilante leader. Look at his shoes. No wonder he didn't want to show them!"

Smiley knelt and examined the heels. "You're right, Race! There's the suction cups, and there's the one that's caked with mud. This is the heel that left the impression in that pitch!"

Ed nodded and said bitterly, "Yes. Art Jennings' own body-guard. Krane had the connection in New York, and he got those gangsters to come here and pose as Vigilantes. He probably got some shyster lawyer in New York to make that offer of fifty thousand. He was using the money that he had made from Art Jennings to buy out his boss!"

"It looks," Captain Smiley said slowly, "as if this is the end of the Vigilante scare in Harmonville. I guess Jennings will be happy to hear it when you tell him."

"You can go and tell him, Cap," Ed said. "I've got to rehearse for tonight's show." He added: "And listen—try to keep my name out of the paper, will you? If Mr. Partages hears that I've been giving some more free shooting exhibitions, he'll fire me off the circuit!"

ACTION OFF STAGE

THE SIGN on the railroad station said:

KIRKVILLE, KENTUCKY
Louisville, 150 mi.

Ed Race was the only passenger arriving this evening, and before he had well put his feet on the platform the conductor signaled ahead, and the locomotive *whiffed,* yanked the train away like a disgusted mother dragging little Willie from in front of the cage of a smelly animal at the zoo.

Ed watched the train pull away, regretfully. He eyed the warmly lit dining car at which men and women were enjoying well-prepared food; then when the train had gone, leaving its faint rumble along the tracks, he turned a bilious eye on what there was to see of the thriving town of Kirkwood, Kentucky.

Three men were lounging around the doorway of the express office. They wore patched trousers and open vests over dirty-looking khaki shirts. Two boys were playing tick-tac-toe with chalk on the platform right under the window of the ticket office. All five seemed to be looking Ed Race over in a furtive sort of way, but they all avoided his eye when he glanced at them.

He picked up his bag and strode through the ticket office to the street.

Parked in front of the station were three cars—a 1928 Buick with a hack license pasted in the windshield, a 1926 Chevrolet whose roof was almost half off, and a brand new 1936 Cadillac sedan. Main Street ran at right angles from the street on which the station was located, and Ed, from where he stood, could look down its entire length of perhaps three blocks.

Electric light signs stretched all the way down, and he read the big ones. There was the Kirkwood Hotel—tourists accommodated, rooms by the day, week or season. There was the Kirkwood Theater, where Ed was bound for, and he could read the poster on the sandwich sign under the marquee, which carried the announcement of his own appearance starting tomorrow:

By Special Arrangement—for One Week Beginning Monday, December 9th—
THE MASKED MARKSMAN
In Person!
See the greatest attraction of the vaudeville stage, direct from New York and Chicago. THE MASKED MARKSMAN—The Man Who Can Make Guns Talk—will appear in person on the stage of the Kirkwood Theater, and give the same performance for which New York and Chicago audiences paid Two Dollars.
25c—Admission—25c

Ed grimaced. If anyone but Leon Partages, the boss of the Partages Circuit, had asked Ed Race to accept a week's booking in a one-horse town on a subway circuit, Ed would have raised the roof and quit cold. But there were a lot of things that Ed Race would do for fat, generous Leon Partages that he wouldn't

do for anyone else; and he was certain that there was something more than a whim behind Partages' telegraphed request.

Strange as it seemed, the driver of the Buick taxi did not approach Ed and solicit him as a fare. On the contrary, the taxi man sat stolidly behind the wheel and glanced everywhere but in Ed's direction.

Instead, the door of the shiny new Cadillac sedan opened, and two men emerged. One of them was dressed in a tight-waisted gray tweed suit that spread around the shoulders so that it almost opened at the seams. His face was broad and flat, and the lips were thick. Small eyes peered at Ed from under a low-visored cap. Ed could see the bulge in the tweed jacket where the man carried a shoulder holster; and Ed himself instinctively hunched his own shoulders forward so as to nudge the twin holsters under his own armpits, where nestled the two heavy forty-five caliber hair-trigger revolvers, mates of the other four in the suitcase.

Those six revolvers went wherever Ed Race went. They were the mainstays of his gun-juggling act. With them, he had performed the amazing feats of marksmanship on the stage that had brought him headline rating in the vaudeville circuits of the country....

HE PUT the suitcase down when he saw that the tweed-suited man and his companion were coming in his direction. He let his hands swing free at his sides and waited for them. Leon Partages' telegram had hinted at trouble, but it had been very circumspect. Ed was prepared for anything—except what actually happened now.

The companion of the big fellow in tweeds was a small, wizened man of fifty-odd, with a sharp nose and big ears that stuck out at right angles from a long head. He wore no hat, and the top of his skull was shiny and clean. He wore a pair of overalls over a vest and trousers; and pinned to one of the straps of his overalls was a nickel badge bearing the words, engraved in a semi-circle halfway around a star:

SHERIFF—HAWK COUNTY

He glanced sideways at the big man, then looked at Ed and said: "Excuse me. Is you-all's name Edward Race?"

Ed nodded. His body was taut, his hands ready for a lightning dive to his armpit holsters at the first overt act of the tweed-suited one. "I'm Ed Race," he said. "Why?"

ACTION OFF STAGE

The sheriff's long face grew even longer. He shook his head deprecatingly and said to the man in tweeds: "Call your datter, Bixby."

The big man glared at Ed, turned to the sedan and raised his voice. "Come on outen thar, Effie!"

Ed watched the proceedings, puzzled. He saw the door of the Cadillac sedan open once more. A slim, pretty, red-haired girl of eighteen or nineteen got out of the car. She wore a flowered, gingham dress under a tan coat which was open at the throat. Her eyes were large, round, and she appeared to be very nervous.

She shivered a little, closed the door of the car behind her, and came slowly toward them. She wore no stockings, and her cheap shoes shuffled along the pavement.

Bixby said to her: "Is this the man what tried to get funny with you out on the post road yestiddy, Effie?"

Her gaze flitted to Ed's face, then dropped to the ground. "Y-yes," she said, very low, very huskily. Then she went on as if repeating a lesson she had learned by rote: "I—I wuz walkin' fur a little air, an' this man come along an' tried to grab me, an' I got scairt an' run back to town. He chased me a while, but I run faster'n him."

She stopped talking, bit her lip hard, and looked sullenly at Bixby. Bixby glowed, nodded in satisfaction. "So that's the man!"

"Just one minute!" Ed Race said softly, dangerously. "I think I understand the game. If this young lady claims she saw me outside of town yesterday, she's either mistaken or lying. I just came in on the train from Louisville. Half a dozen people saw me get off. Here—" He turned to the three or four loafers who

131

had been around the express office, and who had followed him out to the street. "These men will tell you they saw me get off—"

He stopped, his eyes narrowing, as all three of them started to shake their heads in negation. Finally one of them said, speaking to the sheriff: "We didn't see nothin' Abel. Nobody come off thet thar train!"

BIXBY EXCLAIMED triumphantly: "There! You're lyin', mister. You're the one what made the pass at my Effie last night. Abel—" he gestured toward the sheriff "— do your duty!"

The sheriff said morosely: "I'm arrestin' you, mister, fer bein' a public noosance. You better come quiet—"

Ed's face had gone a dull brick red. "If you think you can pull a raw frame like this on me—"

The sheriff's eyes were small, menacing. "You better not get nasty, mister. It don't pay to resist an officer. I got deputies." He waved his hand toward the three loafers who had just denied seeing anybody get off the train. They had produced big, old-fashioned revolvers, and were pointing them at Ed.

Ed glanced at them, then turned his gaze back, let it flick over Bixby and his daughter, then settle on the sheriff. Ed's mouth was a thin, grim line, and his eyes were bleak. He had heard of things like this being done. For some reason, these men wanted to get him out of the way. They would put him in the local jail, and later in the night a mob would gather, sadistic, crazed at the thought of a stranger attempting to attack one of their local girls. They would storm the jail, take the prisoner out and string him up. There might be an investigation later, but nothing would come of it. And Ed Race, the Masked Marksman, would be dead. There must be something of great importance at stake here in Kirkwood, for them to have planned such an elaborate reception for him.

The sheriff had produced a pair of handcuffs. "The boys'd shoot you as soon as spit," he said. "Better put out your hands—"

"Sure," Ed said mildly. "I'm certain that you will find that Miss Bixby is mistaken. Do you mind if I get Mr. Billings, the manager of the Kirkwood Theater? I'd like to have him arrange bail."

Bixby, standing next to the sheriff, grinned nastily. "Billings is in the hoosegow, too. You an' him can get together."

"I see," Ed said, very low. He had come closer to the sheriff, whose small eyes were lighting triumphantly as he stretched out the handcuffs. Ed's body tautened. His steel-spring muscles, hardened by years of practice in his acrobatic gun-juggling act, responded now with the speed of lightning.

His left hand flicked out, seized the sheriff by the front of his overalls. The other, moving with eye-defying swiftness, snaked out one of the heavy forty-fives from a shoulder holster.

Almost in the same motion, Ed swiveled around, swinging the suddenly white-face sheriff so that that functionary was between himself and the guns of the three deputies. The deputies gaped, open-mouthed. The whole thing had happened before their slow-moving wits could grasp the situation.

Not so, Bixby. The big man cursed, and took a step toward Ed, reaching at the same time for his gun. Ed kicked out sideways, caught him in the left shin with the toe of his right shoe, and Bixby let out a howl, doubling over in agony. Ed's kick had been far from gentle. The big man dropped his gun and used both hands to massage his shin, groaning with the pain.

Ed grinned into the sheriff's face, which was less than an inch from his own. He dug the forty-five into the sheriff's stomach, and released his hold on the overalls. "Now, Abel," Ed said gently, "suppose you turn around—very slow!"

The sheriff gulped, gasped: "Y-you wouldn't shoot. You'd hev the law onto you!"

ED SAID: "That's what *you* think, Abel," and moved his gun over to one side so that the barrel lay against the sheriff's ribs, with the muzzle pointing just past him, at the air. Then he pulled the trigger.

The big gun bucked, roared, and the slug tore through the cloth of the sheriff's coat and ricocheted off the ground. The sheriff screamed, thinking he'd been hit, and started to jump away, but Ed caught him by the shoulder, swung him around to face the deputies. Then he put his arm around the sheriff's neck from behind, yanked him backward, still using him as a shield against the three guns of the yokels.

He backed past the girl, Effie, who was standing there rooted to the ground in terror, then he stepped quickly back past the Cadillac, reached over and pulled open the door of the Buick.

The taxi driver had been watching the swift action with startled eyes. Now he yelled: "Hey, there—!" But he shut his mouth tight as Ed stepped back into the rear of his car, dragged the sheriff in with him, and slammed the door.

"Get going, brother," Ed said coldly to the driver. He flung the sheriff to the floor in front of him, planted his foot in the small of his back.

The three deputies were advancing cautiously toward the Buick, afraid to shoot lest they harm Abel. The driver of the Buick turned around to face Ed and said shakily, with a crafty look in his eye: "This car ain't runnin'. There's something wrong with the ignition—"

Ed clucked sympathetically. "That's too bad, brother. They can mark your tombstone: 'Junked because of faulty ignition!'"

The driver paled. "W-what—?"

"I mean," Ed told him matter-of-factly, "that I'm going to put a slug right between your ears—if this car isn't going inside of two seconds!"

The driver looked into Ed's gray, bleak eyes, and hastily turned front, stepped on the starter.

Looking back out the rear window, Ed saw Bixby, still nursing his shin; saw the girl, Effie, standing and staring after him with parted lips.

Ed grinned thinly, turned to face forward, and looked down at the wriggling form of the sheriff. He pressed down more firmly with his foot, and Abel stopped wriggling.

They were passing the marquee of the Kirkwood Theater, and Ed noticed, glancing across the street, that there was an old building, boarded up, that had apparently also been a theater at one time. Across the facade of the building he could make out the lettering:

BIXBY'S MAMMOTH THEATER

135

His eyes lit up in understanding....

The driver asked over his shoulder: "W-where you want me to go?"

"Just keep going," Ed ordered. "I'll tell you where to turn, and when to stop."

They passed a low, one-story brick building with bars on the windows, and Ed read the bronze plate alongside the door:

HAWK COUNTY COURT HOUSE AND JAIL

He made a mental note of its location, and then the car had sped past the last building on Main Street and they were out on the open road.

Ed said pleasantly to the sheriff: "You can get up now, Abel. I want to talk."

ABEL GOT to his knees, looked up venomously at Ed. He was still holding on to the handcuffs. "You done fixed yourself up plenty fine!" he said with spiteful satisfaction. "Now you-all is a fugitive from justice. You-all will be shot on sight when the posse comes after you!"

"That's better than being strung up by the neck by a lynching mob, Abel. Now maybe you'll tell me why you staged that crazy frame back at the station?"

The sheriff got up sullenly and seated himself on the upholstered seat beside Ed, who still held the forty-five negligently in his hand. Abel said nothing.

Ed grinned tightly. "Won't talk, eh? All right, Abel." He glanced out the window, saw that they were passing a roadside restaurant. A hundred feet further on, they passed a side road leading into a landscaped park. Ed called out to the driver: "Hold it, brother!"

The driver braked to a stop, and Ed said: "Back up to that side road."

The taxi man started to obey, and the sheriff said: "Don't you do it, Hank. This here fella is bluffin'. He won't shoot you."

The driver shoved his gear shift into reverse and backed up. "Lissen, Abel," he said over his shoulder, "I ain't aimin' to meet no early death. Effen you thinks he won't shoot, why, you're welcome to start up within him. Me, I don't like the look in his eye!"

Ed grinned. "Smart boy, Hank. Stop right here. Now pull into that side road."

The driver obeyed. It was quite dark here among the trees, and when the car was pulled in to a considerable distance, Ed poked Abel with his gun, ordered: "Get in the front seat with Hank. And if you think I'm bluffing, now is the time for you to find out."

The sheriff got in front. Ed took the handcuffs, linked Hank's right hand and Abel's left hand to the steering wheel, delved in the sheriff's pockets and confiscated an automatic and a set of keys. He also took the ignition keys out of the lock, pocketed them and said pleasantly: "If you two gentlemen will sit here quietly for an hour or so, I'll be obliged."

He winked at them, started away. A few feet away he thought of something, turned back. He stepped to the front of the car, lifted the hood, and felt around till he touched the wire leading to the horn. He yanked this hard, and it came away in his

137

hand. "I bet," Ed remarked to the sheriff, "you were telling Hank what a damn' fool I was, and that you could get help in a couple of minutes by blowing the horn! Too bad, Abel. You'll have to figure out another one!"

Neither of them said anything as Ed left them, tramping back to the roadside restaurant they had passed....

There were no cars at the stand when Ed reached it, and the restaurant part was closed up. The man in charge of the stand was at the rear, fiddling with a radio. He glanced up at Ed, apparently annoyed at the prospect of the interruption, and came to the counter. He was a lanky chap, and his hair was parted exactly in the center, glossed back with some sort of hair-glue. He glared and said, "Yes?"

Ed bought a bottle of ginger ale, drank half of it, and asked the man, "Can I use your 'phone?"

There was a coin-box just inside, and Ed nodded toward it.

The man was suspicious. People don't ordinarily walk up to a roadside stand—they drive up. He said grudgingly, "Go ahead. You can come in through the side door."

ED WALKED around to the door, entered, and saw the man significantly fingering an automatic which he had taken out of a drawer. Ed grinned at him. "It's all right," he said, "I'm not a hold-up. The car is down the road a bit—something wrong with the steering wheel."

The man grunted, went over to the radio and started fiddling with it again, but didn't turn his back.

Ed took out a pocketful of change, inserted a nickel in the slot of the 'phone, and asked for long distance.

ACTION OFF STAGE

The operator said she would call him when she got Mr. Part-ages, and Ed hung up, leaning against the wall idly to watch the man at the radio. There was some static coming through, and only raucous sounds could be heard.

Automobile tires crunched gravel outside, and Ed saw a small coupé pull up in front of the stand. The man at the radio looked up and called out: "Hello, Joe!" to the newcomer. Ed knew why the next moment, when he saw the uniformed State Trooper getting out.

The State Trooper stretched, patted the holstered revolver at his side, and leaned against the counter, tilting his hat back from his forehead. " 'Lo, Sam," he said to the counterman. "Gimme a hamburger. Fry it hard, and put plenty onions on it."

"Okay," said Sam.

The trooper glanced toward Ed, inquiringly, and Sam told him: "This here gent is stuck down the road a piece—something wrong with his steering."

"Yeah?" said the trooper. "Where?"

Ed jerked his thumb down the road.

"That's funny," the trooper replied, frowning. "I just come from that way. Didn't see any car."

"I pulled it off the road," Ed told him, "to avoid accidents."

The 'phone rang, and Ed picked up the receiver. Partages' voice came to him from the other end, in New York City:

"Hello, hello! Who's—?"

"Hello, Mr. Partages," Ed said into the instrument, trying to keep his voice as low as possible. "This is Ed."

"Hello, Eddie boy! I been worried—"

"Listen, Mr. Partages," Ed interrupted. "Why did you send me to Kirkwood? I'm being pushed around here, and I don't even know who's who—"

"You see Billings," Partages broke in. "He's my manager over at the Kirkwood Theater. He'll tell you everything—"

Over the sound of Partages' voice, there came to Ed's ears another voice. It was cold, crisp, and it was coming from the radio!

"State Police Barracks calling Troopers Williamson, Casey and Olivier.... Arrest on sight, one Edward Race, vaudeville actor known as the Masked Marksman. Last seen driving south along Highway Twenty-three—two-three—in commandeered Buick taxi. He assaulted a girl and kidnapped the sheriff of Hawk County from in front of the Kirkwood Railroad Station. Use extreme caution. Race is an expert marksman, and is armed. He is five feet ten, weighs about one hundred and ninety. Fair hair, gray eyes, square jaw. When last seen, was wearing a gray suit and topcoat, and a gray felt hat. Trooper Williamson particularly, watch Highway Twenty-three.... I will repeat—State Police Barracks calling cars...."

OUT OF the corner of his eye Ed could see the trooper at the counter staring at him appraisingly.

Ed said hurriedly into the 'phone, "I'll call you later, Mr. Partages. Got some pressing business now." He hung up, and even as he did so his right hand streaked to his holster in a motion so fast that it was almost imperceptible to the eye. It came out with one of the forty-fives, and Ed covered the trooper and the counterman before the trooper's hand could come up again from the holster at his waist. "Keep it low!" Ed warned.

The counterman exclaimed: "Hully-gee! I knowed he was a phony!"

The trooper did not lift the gun from his holster. He stood rigid under the muzzle of Ed's gun, but there was a glint of unwilling admiration in his eyes. "That was the fastest draw I ever saw in my life," he said. "You must be the Masked Marksman, all right."

Ed climbed over the counter, keeping both men covered. Then he said to the counterman, "You, too. Come on over."

The counterman hesitated, glanced at the trooper, then gulped and climbed over. Ed marched the two of them around to the back of the building and into the closed-up part where the restaurant was located.

Ed made the counterman lie down on the floor, and then waved his gun at the trooper. "Tie him up with those towels!"

The trooper remonstrated. "You're only making things worse for yourself by this, Race."

"Tie him up!" Ed repeated.

The trooper shrugged, picked up a batch of dish towels from a rack, twisted them, and tied the counterman's hands. When he was finished, Ed tried the knots to be sure they were firm, then said to the trussed-up man, "Don't worry, Sam. You won't be here long. We'll come back and let you go."

Sam only glared, but the trooper looked surprised. "*We?*" he asked.

Ed nodded, grinned. "You and I are going places, Joe. Come on."

Joe's homely face expressed puzzlement. "You ain't goin' to tie me up here, too?"

"No. And you can keep your gun, too. Let's go."

They left the counterman, moved around to the front of the building. Ed rummaged around till he found a piece of cardboard from a carton, gave the trooper a pencil, and ordered:

"Print on that: 'This stand is on a self-service basis. Please help yourself and leave correct change on counter.'"

The trooper grinned, obeyed, printing the words with a flourish. Then, at Ed's direction, he tacked the sign up to the front of the stand.

"This will be a good test of people's honesty," Ed told him. "It's always been my contention that people are inherently honest. I bet our friend Sam doesn't lose a nickel by this."

"I think you're nuts," the trooper said glumly. "What do we do now—dance a jig or something?"

"No," Ed informed him. "We drive back to Kirkwood—in your car!"

The trooper stared at him a moment, then exclaimed: "Well, I'll be damned!"

IT WAS two-and-a-half miles back to Kirkwood, and the trooper drove slowly, a puzzled look on his face. Ed sat beside him and put his forty-five back in the shoulder holster. "What's your last name, Joe?" he asked.

"Williamson. Look here, Race, I don't get you. I saw your act in Louisville last week. I can't figure how you fit into a mess like this. You know you can't get away. Sooner or later you'll be corralled. You ain't going to give up your career on the stage an' everything?"

"You're right," Ed said.

"Then what're you taking me into Kirkwood for? If you want to make a fool of me—"

"Look," said Ed. "I'm not taking you into Kirkwood. You're taking me. Here's my gun!" He held out his forty-five.

A look of amazement spread over the trooper's face. "You givin' yourself up?" He took one hand from the wheel, accepted the gun, and glanced sideways at Ed. "Then what'd you pull that fast play back at the roadstand for?"

"Because I sized you up as a regular guy and I wanted a chance to talk to you in private. Slow up a little, so I can tell you a story."

The trooper let up on the accelerator, hugged the side of the road. "Shoot!"

For ten minutes Ed talked earnestly, tensely. "Will you take a chance and play along with me?" he finished.

For a moment the trooper hesitated. Then he picked up Ed's gun from his lap, where he had laid it, and handed it back. "Here's your gun, Race," he said.

"Good man!" Ed said softly.

MAIN STREET was crowded with Sunday night pleasure-seekers from the surrounding countryside. Cars were parked in an unbroken line at both curbs, all the way down to the station.

Ed pulled his hat low over his face as Williamson drove past the county jail. He didn't stop, but drove down the side street, turned left again at the next corner, and pulled up before the rear entrance of the jail. Ed gave him the bunch of keys he had taken from the sheriff, and the trooper got out, fitted one into the door and went in.

A few minutes later someone shouted inside, and there was the sound of a blow.

Soon the door opened and Williamson came out, half supporting a short, stout man who appeared disheveled, unkempt. He breathed the fresh air eagerly and hastily ran over to the coupé, where he gripped Ed's hand and shook it.

Williamson came up behind him and said to Ed, "Here's Billings, Race. I had to knock out a jailer to free him." He chuckled. "Imagine State Trooper Williamson conniving in a jailbreak!"

Billings turned, patted Williamson on the shoulder. "You won't regret this, Joe. I'll see you're plenty taken care of!"

He swung on Ed. "They slammed me around. It was my wife 'phoned Mr. Partages in New York. She threw me a note in the window, saying Mr. Partages was sending you here from Louisville. I—"

"Wait a minute, Billings." Ed got out of the car, while Williamson watched up and down the street. "What's been happening here? Who wanted you to close the Kirkwood?"

"Bixby," the manager told Ed. "When I took over the Kirkwood for Mr. Partages, Bixby had to close down."

"I get it," Ed said. "So he had the sheriff go to work on you."

Billings nodded. "They came in the cell and grabbed the note my wife threw in, almost before I'd finished reading it, so they knew you were coming. I was afraid they'd put you in jail, too."

"They almost did," Ed said grimly. He looked at Williamson. "What do you think now, Joe? Were you a sucker to play along with me?"

Williamson grinned. "I think Bixby will be the sucker!" he said. "But right now, the three of us ain't so hot. Billings here is a fugitive from the county jail; I aided him to escape; and you're wanted for assault on a girl, an' for abductin' the sheriff—and God knows for what else!"

"I think," Ed said bleakly, "that the next step indicated is a little informal call on the Honorable Mr. Bixby!"

"I know where he lives," Billings said.

BUT THEY didn't call on Mr. Bixby. Mr. Bixby called on them. Ed glanced down the street, suddenly grabbed Billings and pushed him into the car, scrambled in himself. "The girl!" he exclaimed to Williamson. "Get out of sight!"

The girl, Effie Bixby, had just turned the corner and was standing there uncertainly, the light from a street lamp shining in her face. Williamson ducked back into the doorway of the jail, and they watched her. Ed crowded close beside Billings, who murmured: "Wonder what she wants around here? She's Bixby's stepdaughter. He treats her something terrible. Effie's own mother, who was Bixby's second wife, is dead, and she's got no place to go, so she has to stay and take his guff."

Ed grunted, watched through the back window of the car. Effie Bixby stood on the corner for a moment, as if gathering her courage, then started down the street toward the jail entrance. She had only taken a few steps when the big Cadillac that Ed had seen at the station rounded the corner behind her, pulled up at the curb alongside her. The door opened, and Bixby got out. The girl had stopped upon hearing the car. Now she shrank back against the wall of the building as if in physical fear of her stepfather.

Bixby stood over her, and Ed could see his face, convulsed with anger. He was staring down at the girl, and all he said was, "Crossing me, eh?"

The girl had a hand at her mouth, and she was pressing her frail body as far back as she could get. Bixby's big hand came up, open, swung hard against the girl's cheek, and she uttered a little gasp. Bixby snarled, "What you doing here?"

Effie had covered her face with her hands. She was sobbing. "I—I can't go through with it!" she moaned. "They'll—they'll hunt that poor Mr. Race, and k-kill him. I—I was going to tell Mr. Billings all about it."

"Oh!" said Bixby. "So you were going to tell Billings all about it!" He gripped her shoulder so that she winced. "You come back to the house with me!"

Ed Race was out of the police coupé and running up the street toward them, his face bleak and gray. Bixby saw him coming, and he held the girl close to himself, tugging at the gun in his shoulder holster. His face was lit up as the gun came out. But he never fired….

Ed's big forty-five was out and bucking in his hand to the echo of its thunderous explosion. The slug from the forty-five creased Bixby's right arm, and the big man dropped his gun, screaming.

He let go his grip on the girl, pushed her aside, and stooped, picked up the gun again with his left hand. Ed could have shot him once more, but he didn't. His momentum as he ran carried him to within a foot of Bixby as the man straightened.

Ed's forty-five came down with stunning force on Bixby's left wrist. At the same time, Ed's left fist crashed up in a short, vicious arc to the point of Bixby's jaw, and the big man collapsed.

Williamson and Billings came running up, and Ed bent, helping Effie Bixby to her feet. She clung to him, her eyes wet. "Y-you must t-thing me—awful—for telling that lie back at the station!"

Ed smiled, patted her shoulder. "No, kid. That guy had you buffaloed. You couldn't do anything else. You had guts to come here now, this way."

She smiled contentedly. "I—I'm glad you don't think I'm—wicked." She glanced down at Williamson, who was bending over the unconscious Bixby, and she shuddered. "W-what are you going to do—with him?"

"There's no charge against him," Ed said gloomily. "He's kept within the law."

Billings asked uncertainly, "You—you think it'll be all right for me to open the Kirkwood now?"

"Sure." Ed grinned. "And you've got a new cashier." He pushed Effie Bixby forward. "From now on, she works for you. You give her an advance so she can get herself some place to live."

"I'll do better than that," Billings said, beaming. "I'll take her home. Mrs. Billings'll be glad to have her live with us!"

THERE WAS a glad light in Effie's eyes as she beamed her

thanks at both of them. Ed turned away, said gruffly to William-son, "Come on. Let's bundle Bixby in your car and go places."

"What places?" the trooper asked.

"We have to untie a couple of people that I left around, out on the road. And—see how many nickels Sam the counterman took in on the self-service system!"

PROLOGUE TO DEATH

NEW YORK in January. Men with their overcoat collars turned up, and their hands dug deep in their pockets, plodding through dirty sleet, and shivering in the first blasts of a freezing spell that would turn the sleet to ice by morning; women in swanky fur coats, with their necks exposed, wearing sheer silk stockings and low shoes, and not seeming to mind the weather at all, as long as they could look attractive.

Ed Race, walking down Broadway from the Longmont Hotel, where he had just checked in from a Midwest vaudeville tour, liked it all, in spite of the depressing weather.

The smells and the noise and the crowds of New York were like a revivifying breath in his nostrils after six months in the Hinterland. He was a New Yorker. It was born and bred in him. He knew the Main Stem, knew its frailties, its wickednesses, its joys and its sorrows—He knew everybody, and everybody knew him. Already he had nodded to half a dozen acquaintances. They took his presence on Broadway for granted. No doubt they had already seen the big electric sign on the marquee of the Clyde Theater, two blocks down, announcing his return vaudeville engagement.

Ed could see it from the corner of Forty-sixth, which he had just crossed:

THE MASKED MARKSMAN

Return engagement! Beginning tonight!
THE MASKED MARKSMAN
THE MAN WHO CAN MAKE GUNS TALK!

At the Nedick stand on the south corner, Ed saw Lou Donner, the *Daily Express* columnist, having a frankfurter and a glass of orangeade. Lou Donner generally looked Ed up whenever the actor returned to town. The genial little columnist always got a few lines for his paper out of Ed, and Ed liked him. He wondered why Lou hadn't been around to the Longmont, and he pushed through the evening theater-going crowd to the Nedick stand, came up behind Donner, and said:

"Hello, Louie. Still eating hot dogs! Why don't you blow yourself to a regular meal one of these days?"

Donner turned around. He wore big shell-rimmed glasses because he was nearsighted, and he blinked at Ed while he swallowed a mouthful of frankfurter and roll. He still had half of it in his hand, uneaten. He exclaimed: "Why, Eddie! Glad to see you, Eddie!" But he didn't offer to shake hands. Instead, he looked around nervously, put down his frankfurter, fished hastily in his pocket for a dime, and slapped it on the counter. "I got to beat it, Eddie. See you soon!" And he was gone through the crowd....

Ed stared after him, astounded. He had expected a different sort of welcome from the little columnist, for whom he had done many a favor in the past. He glanced down, puzzled, at the unfinished hot dog and the almost full glass of orange drink; shrugged and continued down Broadway.

At the next corner, Ed saw Kolman, the bookie. Kolman had his stand at the corner of Forty-fifth and Broadway. It was his

unofficial office. If you had won a bet from him that day, you could come to that corner in the evening and collect. He had been paying off at that same spot for ten years now, and he was a Broadway institution.

He saw Ed at the same time that Ed saw him, and the bookie's square, usually expressionless face lighted up in welcome. But as soon as Ed started toward him, the smile fled from Kolman's face, gave place to a look of uneasiness. He took Ed Race's outstretched hand, allowed his own to be shaken.

"I—I heard you was back in town, Ed," he said. "It's sure good to see you again. Well, I got to scram. Can't make no dough here. Ha-ha! Well, so long, Ed!" He practically tore his hand away from Ed's and hastened around the corner....

ED STOOD there for a second, frowning, being jostled by the crowd. First Donner, then Kolman. It was as if he had the plague. There was something wrong in town—something which Ed Race felt he should know. He had made plenty of enemies in his career; for he wasn't merely a headline vaudeville actor who had pushed through to top rank by virtue of his amazing skill with revolvers on the stage. His nervous energy had demanded greater thrill, greater excitement than the routine of shooting out candles on the stage, of juggling heavy forty-fives and shooting with such amazing precision as to bring down the house at every performance. And that nervous energy had found an adequate outlet in the sideline of crime detection, which Ed Race had pursued for several years now. He held licenses as a private detective in a dozen states; and his ability with six-guns had often served his friends—but it had also made him some deadly foes.

Now he nudged his side with his left arm, so as to bring slightly forward the holster under his left armpit, in which nestled one of the six forty-fives with which he performed on the stage. Under his right armpit there was another holster, in which rested a twin to that gun. The other four would be at the Clyde Theater, carefully wrapped in chamois, ready for the act.

PROLOGUE TO DEATH

They had been shipped through direct, with his other stage properties.

There might and might not be danger, but Ed Race had learned that it is better to be careful than dead. His body tautened slightly, and he started to cross Forty-fifth.

He was in the middle of the crossing, with dozens of other people slushing through the sleet in an effort to get over before the light changed, when the woman screamed.

The woman had been crossing in the opposite direction, coming toward Ed, and her right foot was just off the curb when she uttered the scream. She pointed with a shaking finger at something out in the street on Broadway, above the corner, and turned to push frantically back into the throng behind her. Ed Race swung his head, saw what had made her scream....

It was a beautiful, maroon sedan of streamline design. It was crawling down past the red light, and its right front window was open. Out of that window poked the unmistakable snout of a submachine gun. And that snout was pointed right at the press of the crowd about Ed Race.

Even as Ed looked, the tommy began to chatter and belch lead. The burst sounded high above the noises of Broadway, smashed into the crowd, mowing down half a dozen people at the crossing. Ed could see that the gunner in the car was working the gun around toward where he stood. And Ed's body swung into sudden blinding, synchronized motion.

Into his two hands came the two heavy, hair-trigger forty-fives. While men and women ran, slipping and stumbling madly through the sleet to escape that withering barrage of death, Ed

Race stood his ground, spraddle-legged in the middle of the crossing. His two revolvers were talking in deep-throated angry roar almost before the first burst from the tommy had begun to echo. They bucked in his hands as flame spat from their muzzles into the open window of the maroon sedan.

Abruptly, the submachine gun ceased to chatter, its snout dropped, a bloody face appeared in the window, and the gun fell out into the gutter. The motor of the sedan roared as the driver accelerated, and the car sped south against the light. But Ed did not cease firing. Bleak-eyed, tight-lipped, he swung his two guns after the fleeing car, swiveling his body from the hips....

HE JUST had a glimpse of the driver's head through that open window, past the sagging head of the machine-gunner, which rested against the sill of the window. And that glimpse was enough for Ed. The driver's hands fell from the wheel as a slug smashed into the side of his head. The sedan careened wildly, lurched to the left, and crashed against the concrete island in the middle of Broadway.

It jumped the curb, ended up against the subway kiosk with a rending, crashing sound of twisting metal. Flames leaped from it as it turned over.

Broadway was in pandemonium. People came running from everywhere, while Ed Race put away his guns, glanced down at the bloody shambles at his feet. Six men and women had been caught by that first burst from the tommy gun. They lay in the gutter, spattered with blood and sleet and mud. Four were motionless, dead. Two stirred, twisted and moaned.

Policemen appeared, and an ambulance siren sounded; a radio

car squealed to a stop at the corner. Fire engines swung into Broadway from Forty-sixth, and their crews ran to the burning sedan with the chemical extinguishers.

A stocky, heavy-set man came up to Ed Race, put a hand on his shoulder. It was Detective-Sergeant Bland, of Homicide.

Ed said to him: "Hello, Steve. You missed the fun." There was no smile on his lips as he said it, and his eyes were bleak, cold.

Bland, white-lipped, exclaimed: "My God, Race, I saw the whole thing from down the block, but I was too far to shoot. It's wholesale murder! Why the hell did you have to show yourself in the street? Didn't you know something like this would happen?"

Ed looked at him blankly, while internes carried the two still living victims from the street into ambulances, and while the firemen fought the flames in the maroon sedan.

"What do you mean, Steve? Why should I expect something like this to happen?"

Bland threw him a queer glance. "You just got back to New York, didn't you?"

Ed nodded.

"And you don't know what's going on in town?"

"I don't know a damn thing. Except that Partages left a message for me at the Longmont to come to the theater as soon as I checked in—and that none of my old friends on Broadway seemed to want to have any part of me. They all made themselves scarce the minute they saw me."

"Of course they would. They must have thought you knew all about it. And they must have thought you were crazy to come out in the street alone like this."

"I wish you'd tell me what it's about."

"Wait a minute," Bland muttered, starting across the street toward the overturned sedan, from which the white-coated internes were dragging two charred bodies. "I want to see if there's enough left of those bozos to identify them."

Ed accompanied the detective-sergeant across to the shattered car, leaning crazily against the subway kiosk. The fire had been extinguished, permitting the ambulance men to remove the two occupants and lay them on the sidewalk. The face of one of them was blistered to a pulp, unrecognizable; but the other was practically unmarred. There was a bullet wound in the back of the head, where Ed's slug had caught him.

Bland leaned over them, then straightened and turned to Ed. "Just as I thought," he said. "That one is Mickey Tate. You know Mickey Tate?"

Ed nodded. "He's one of French Hugo's mob, if my memory serves me. But"—he looked puzzled—"what would French Hugo have against me? He may have all the rackets in Harlem sewed up, but he's never tangled with me. Why would he send a crew gunning for me the minute I get back to town—and why would everybody know about it but me?"

BLAND SIGHED. "Look, Race," he said, "you work for the Partages Vaudeville Circuit, but you've been out of town for six months, so you're a little dusty on the inside dope. Shortly after you left town, French Hugo moved down to Broadway. He's been collecting from every theater on the Main Stem—except from Mr. Partages' houses. Now he's gone after your boss for fair—and it's almost impossible for the police to give him protection."

"Nice boy, Hugo," Ed said drily. "Why don't you pick him up?"

Bland flushed. "He *has* been picked up—several times. The orders are out to muss him up, and believe me, he *was* mussed up. But there's never anything to hold him on." The detective-sergeant swore softly under his breath. "And every time he's released, something new happens at the Clyde or one of the other Partages Theaters. Your boss is almost ready to give in and pay up."

"Not Leon," Ed told him confidently. "I know Leon Partages. But why wasn't I told about this? Here you let me walk right into the heat—"

"It's like this," Bland informed him wearily. "This morning, when that sign went up on the Clyde announcing your return, Partages got a telephone call. The bozo at the other end warned him to cancel your engagement, or else.... I guess French Hugo has a healthy respect for you. Before the 'phone call, I didn't give your coming a thought; but Hugo must have figured that Partages was bringing you back to help fight him. Well, by this afternoon, all Broadway knew Hugo's crowd was going to be gunning for you—which is why your friends shunned you; they didn't want to be around when the shooting started. I called you at the Longmont, but you had already left."

Ed glanced somberly at the wide cleared space about which the reserves had strung a cordon. The area looked like a battle-field, with stretcher bearers and ambulances, with blood in the gutter coloring the sleet a dirty red.

"Where does French Hugo hang out?"

Bland gave him a short laugh. "Don't be a dope, Ed. French Hugo is downtown in headquarters right now. He's got himself a perfect alibi. He came in an hour ago with his attorney to protest against the brutality of the police. We can't even hold him on this shooting; he'd be out on a writ, and laughing at us up his sleeve!"

A headquarters car had pulled up at the curb across the street, in front of the Astor, and out of it stormed a stocky, red-faced man in a blue overcoat and a gray felt hat, who stood for a moment glaring around at the scene of carnage.

Bland exclaimed: "There's the Inspector. He looks like he's all set to raise hell. Let's go over."

They crossed to the police car, and Bland saluted. "It's the worst yet, Inspector. Four people killed, and two badly wounded. Race, here, got the gunner and the driver of the murder car. One of them is Mickey Tate."

Inspector Hansen nodded, looked somberly at Ed. "I never saw anybody like you, Race," he barked testily, "for starting things. I swear, every time I hear you're in town, I get all set for trouble!"

Ed shrugged. He had never been able to *get* along with the testy old homicide inspector. The two just didn't click. "I apologize, Hansen," he said sourly, "for living. I suppose you'd want me to stay holed up for the rest of my life?"

BLAND INTERRUPTED hastily, trying to stave off an explosion from Hansen: "Race didn't know anything about it, Inspector. And if it hadn't been for his fast shooting, a lot more people might have been killed."

Hansen grunted, slightly mollified. "This'll make nice stuff in the headlines."

"Excuse me, Hansen," Ed broke in. "Will you want me here?" He glanced at his wristwatch. "I'm due to go on at the Clyde in half an hour."

The inspector shook his head. "You're not going on tonight, Race. We don't want any more killings in this city. That mob will be after you more than ever now. What chance would you stand, on the stage before two thousand people, if someone lets loose on you?"

"I'll take that chance, Hansen."

"And I say you won't! It's my business to protect you—like it or not."

"That may be so," Ed told him stubbornly, "but my number goes on at the Clyde tonight, Hugo or no Hugo. I've never missed a curtain call in eight years—and I don't intend to begin now."

He started away. "See you both later."

Hansen put a hand on his arm. "Wait a minute, Race!" he snapped. His eyes traveled across to the wrecked car leaning against the subway kiosk. "You shot the two men in that car, didn't you?"

"That's right. Bland saw it. He'll tell you it was self-defense—"

"Maybe, Race, maybe. But I'm holding you on a technical charge of murder. You won't put on any show tonight!"

Ed's face flushed a brick red. "So *you're* what they call a cop!" he barked. "And all you can do when a thing like this happens is arrest the man who did what your own cops are supposed to do."

Hansen's eyes were blazing, his face was pink, and he was stuttering in apoplectic rage. Steve Bland stepped in between them, put a hand on Ed's shoulder.

"Look, Race," he urged, "the Inspector is only looking out for your own good. It's dollars to doughnuts that someone will be planted in the audience at the Clyde tonight, to finish up what Mickey Tate started here. We can't search everybody buying a ticket to see if they're armed. You could be shot as easy—"

Ed listened to him impatiently, his eyes roving over the crowd at the curb, which was goggling at the scene, and surging against the line of patrolmen holding them back. And he spied the little columnist, Lou Donner, waving to him.

Ed grinned. Donner was anxious to get to him now that the danger seemed over.

Bland was still talking, but Inspector Hansen broke in on him: "Never mind that soft soap, Steve. Race is in custody whether he likes it or not. If he's fool enough not to know he's in a spot—"

Ed Race, still grinning, called out to the patrolman at the point where Lou Donner was standing: "Let that man through." THE PATROLMAN, seeing Ed apparently in conference with the inspector, thought that the order was official, and stepped aside. Lou Donner rushed through, toward them.

Hansen glanced at the little man waddling swiftly over and glared at Ed. "What's the idea, Race?"

Ed smiled at him sweetly. "I'm going to give Lou Donner an interview, Inspector. In tomorrow morning's *Express,* you can read all about the snappy cop who locked up the man that saved a lot of people from getting shot. You'll like it!"

Hansen sputtered, and Donner came up to them. "Say, Ed!" the columnist exclaimed. "Make this exclusive for me, will you? Boy, will this be a whale of a—"

Ed was looking at Hansen. He swung around to Donner. "I've got a swell bit for you, Lou. I know the *Express* likes to slam the police department—"

"Wait!" Hansen interrupted hoarsely. Ed stopped, glancing inquiringly at the inspector. Hansen gulped. There was murder in his eyes. But he said: "All right, Race. You win. You can go. And I hope they get you tonight!"

Ed said quickly: "That's fine, Inspector. I knew you'd see it my way. So long. I'll see you in the morning."

He started away, taking Donner by the arm. "Come on, Lou. I'll give you the story on the way to the Clyde."

"What's that you said about the *Express* knocking the cops, Ed?" Donner asked. "If you got something, they'll play it up big on the editorial page—"

"Nothing, Lou," Ed said. "Forget it."

"You know, Ed," Donner said hesitantly, "you shouldn't hold it against me that I beat it on you back at the Nedick stand. I know about Hugo gunning for you, and I figured you knew about it, too, and were deliberately showing yourself. After all, you can't blame me for getting out of the way fast. They've got me mixed up in this already, more than I want."

"What do you mean?"

"Partages got a note ordering him to turn over fifty grand, and naming three intermediaries. He's to pick one of them. Well, I'm one of the three intermediaries named, and I don't like it at

161

all." His eyes looked big, and his glasses joggled on his nose as he looked up at Ed. "I've heard of intermediaries learning too much by accident. I'm not so old yet—"

ED LAUGHED. "Here's the theater, Lou. I'm short of time, so I'll give you the story fast. You can see me later for more details." He swiftly gave the columnist a picture of what had happened, then left him and went in through the stage entrance of the Clyde. There was a good deal of excitement here, for they had already heard about the shooting. All the actors and stagehands gathered about Ed, hungry for more information, but he pushed through them.

"Is Mr. Partages in his office?"

An electrician nodded, and Ed extricated himself from the group of questioners, made his way upstairs.

At the door marked: *Leon Partages—Private,* Ed rapped hastily and then pushed in without waiting for an invitation.

There were two men in the mahogany-furnished office. Ed's boss sat behind a glass-topped desk, drumming pudgy fingers on the glass. He was frowning worriedly. The other man sat opposite him.

Partages exclaimed: "Eddie! Gosh it's good to see you! My God, that was a narrow escape you had. Those devils—"

He stopped, sighed. "I'm getting too old for this sort of business." He got up from behind the desk, came around and shook hands with Ed, then turned and introduced the other man, who had risen.

"Meet Hugo Larcy, Ed."

Ed started, glanced at the other man. "French Hugo?" he asked.

The other nodded. "That's me." He was as tall as Ed, and heavy, with a square face and a hard-looking jaw. His eyes were wide-spaced, and his black hair was combed straight back from his forehead. It was thinning a bit at the edges.

French Hugo exclaimed: "Look here, Race, I ain't responsible for that shooting outside. I been trying to make the dumb cops believe me, but I know they don't. I came here to convince Mr. Partages."

Ed said coldly: "I suppose you haven't been in back of the racket that's shaking down the Broadway theaters either?"

"Hell!" the big man protested. "You've heard of me, Race. I'm a good businessman, Race, and I'm not sap enough to think I could get away with this."

"Who's doing it, then?" Ed demanded.

Hugo's face was set, hard. "If I ever find out the name of the rat that's laying this at my door, there'll be one rat less in town five minutes later!"

Ed glanced at Partages, who nodded solemnly. "I believe him, Eddie. French Hugo is no fool. He'd be jeopardizing his business uptown—"

"Not only that," Hugo broke in, "but you've been around town a lot, Race, and you ought to know that I never go in for any Valentine's Day stuff. Anybody who does that is loco."

"Well," Ed asked him, "why did you come here?"

HUGO SHRUGGED. "I'm a plain man. I went down to headquarters with my lawyer, and I told them what I just told you. Hansen is a flat-brained bulldog, and he can't see anything but French Hugo. The more I talk, the less they believe me. So I figured I'd try to convince Partages—maybe work with him so's to clear myself. Now that everybody's blaming me, I got an interest in this business."

Ed turned to Partages and Hugo. "My number will be over in twenty minutes—"

Partages shook his head. "No, Eddie boy. If you go on, your number'll be *up*—not *over*. Look at this!"

He reached to his desk, picked up a folded slip of paper.

Ed took the sheet, spread it open, and read while both men watched him:

> We told you what we wanted—fifty grand on the line. You didn't pay, and you sent for the Masked Marksman. Well, we know who he is. If he ever gets to the Clyde alive, he won't leave it alive. Maybe after we take care of your pet gunman, you'll be ready to talk turkey. If you're ready now, turn out the bulbs in the letter 'C' in the word Clyde on your marquee, as a signal, and send the dough as per the instructions we already gave you.

There was no signature to the note.

"I got another letter," Partages explained, "which I turned over to the police. I'm supposed to pick out one of three names they mention as intermediaries, and turn the money over to the one I select. I was really thinking of paying. I was thinking of calling Lou Donner, because he's the only one of the three that I know pretty well—"

Another knock sounded at the door. "You're on in one minute, Mr. Race!"

Ed started out. "Get Lou on the wire!" he told Partages. "Tell him to be here after the act. Maybe we can figure—"

He had the door open, and French Hugo came after him. "If you don't mind," Hugo said, "I'd like to stay in the wings while you do your stuff. I'll keep my eyes on the audience, and"—he tapped a bulge under his armpit—"I can shoot pretty good myself. That is," he added, "if you trust me."

Ed grinned. "Come on, Hugo. It's okay by me!"

The two men hurried downstairs, leaving Partages at the 'phone.

The orchestra was already swinging into the rhythm for Ed's act when they got into the wings. The other actors, sensing something in the air, were all crowded around, watching breathlessly. Ed took the little black mask which a property man handed him, donned it, waved to the others, and stepped out on the stage.

The lights were on, and would stay on.

Ed's number was always performed with the house fully illuminated. In the center of the stage was a small table on which rested four forty-five caliber revolvers like the two he carried. NOW, AS Ed crossed to the table to the accompaniment of thunderous applause, he took out his two holstered revolvers, loaded them.

Then he flipped them into the air, picked up the other four guns one after the other, and sent them up after the first two. He now had all six guns juggling at once. It was child's play to him, and he glanced out of the corner of his eye toward the wing. French Hugo was standing there, his head poked out from behind the drape, peering at the audience. His hand was thrust within his coat.

Now, Ed sent the revolvers sailing high in the air—all six of them—and did a quick back-somersault to the accompaniment of a crashing chord from the orchestra. This was a difficult spot in the routine. But he had done this successfully, thousands of times, and had never missed.

His superbly muscled body swung backward in a graceful arc. He landed on his feet, took a step forward with his hands outstretched, and the first two revolvers came down into them in the most gracefully, perfectly timed bit of juggling ever booked on a vaudeville stage. Without effort he sent all six forty-fives up again, smiling to the scattered applause.

And just then he heard Hugo's hoarse shout: "Hey!"

At the same time, from somewhere in the mezzanine, there came a soft *pop*, and the automatic dropped from Hugo's hand, while the big man seemed to be flung backward against the drop. Blood appeared on his forehead between the eyes.

Ed dived sideways, with two of the guns in his hand, letting the others fall. His eyes caught a flash of flame high up in the rear of the mezzanine, accompanied by another soft *pop*, and a slug dug into the floor of the stage where Ed had been standing a moment ago.

Ed saw a dark shape moving near where he had spied the flash, and he raised his right-hand revolver, fired six times.

The crash of his guns drowned out the orchestra, and, for the first time, the audience realized that this was not part of the act. Here and there a woman screamed, but for the most part they remained rooted to their seats in terror.

Ed came to his feet lithely. There were no more *pops* from the mezzanine. He sprinted across the stage, stopping only a moment to look down at the dead body of French Hugo, who had died in defense of what he considered his reputation....

IN THE aisle, two of the dozen or so policemen who had been stationed in the theater were racing up the stairs, and Ed followed them. In the mezzanine he saw Leon Partages rushing, white-faced, from the upper lobby, and they all ran toward the rear.

There, just at the head of the center aisle, lay a dark, huddled form, clutching a silenced revolver. Forty or fifty patrons were out of their seats, standing in a wide circle, staring at the dead man.

Ed, with Leon and the cops, pushed through, stood looking down at the body. The dead man was on his face, and one of the officers stooped to turn him over.

"Never mind," Ed said in a queer voice.

He glanced at Leon, who nodded and said very low: "God! Lou Donner!"

"Lou Donner!" exclaimed a voice at the fringe of the crowd. Inspector Hansen pushed through, followed by Steve Bland.

"Yes," Ed said bitterly. "He fooled me perfectly. It was he who hired Mickey Tate and the other gunner. He was the one behind this shakedown. He was smart enough to know that French

Hugo would be blamed. And he was on the inside as to what was being done by the police."

Partages exclaimed: "No wonder he had his name in the list of three intermediaries. He knew I wasn't acquainted with the other two, and that I'd turn the money over to him!"

Hansen swore. "And it wasn't French Hugo, after all!"

"If you were a gentleman," Ed told the inspector, "you'd go and apologize."

"Where is he?" Hansen asked.

Ed grinned. "In Hell by now, I guess!"

THE SPIDER

- ❑ #1: The Spider Strikes — $13.95
- ❑ #2: The Wheel of Death — $13.95
- ❑ #3: Wings of the Black Death — $13.95
- ❑ #4: City of Flaming Shadows — $13.95
- ❑ #5: Empire of Doom! — $13.95
- ❑ #6: Citadel of Hell — $13.95
- ❑ #7: The Serpent of Destruction — $13.95
- ❑ #8: The Mad Horde — $13.95
- ❑ #9: Satan's Death Blast — $13.95
- ❑ #10: The Corpse Cargo — $13.95
- ❑ #11: Prince of the Red Looters — $13.95
- ❑ #12: Reign of the Silver Terror — $13.95
- ❑ #13: Builders of the Dark Empire — $13.95
- ❑ #14: Death's Crimson Juggernaut — $13.95
- ❑ #15: The Red Death Rain — $13.95
- ❑ #16: The City Destroyer — $13.95
- ❑ #17: The Pain Emperor — $13.95
- ❑ #18: The Flame Master — $13.95
- ❑ #19: Slaves of the Crime Master — $13.95
- ❑ #20: Reign of the Death Fiddler — $13.95
- ❑ #21: Hordes of the Red Butcher — $13.95
- ❑ #22: Dragon Lord of the Underworld — $13.95
- ❑ #23: Master of the Death-Madness — $13.95
- ❑ #24: King of the Red Killers — $13.95
- ❑ #25: Overlord of the Damned — $13.95
- ❑ #26: Death Reign of the Vampire King — $13.95
- ❑ #27: Emperor of the Yellow Death — $13.95
- ❑ #28: The Mayor of Hell — $13.95
- ❑ #29: Slaves of the Murder Syndicate — $13.95
- ❑ #30: Green Globes of Death — $13.95
- ❑ #31: The Cholera King — $13.95
- ❑ #32: Slaves of the Dragon — $13.95
- ❑ #33: Legions of Madness — $12.95
- ❑ #34: Laboratory of the Damned — $12.95
- ❑ #35: Satan's Sightless Legion — $12.95
- ❑ #36: The Coming of the Terror — $12.95
- ❑ #37: The Devil's Death-Dwarfs — $12.95
- ❑ #38: City of Dreadful Night — $12.95
- ❑ #39: Reign of the Snake Men — $12.95
- ❑ #40: Dictator of the Damned — $12.95
- ❑ #41: The Mill-Town Massacres — $12.95
- ❑ #42: Satan's Workshop — $12.95
- ❑ #43: Scourge of the Yellow Fangs — $12.95
- ❑ #44: The Devil's Pawnbroker — $12.95
- ❑ #45: Voyage of the Coffin Ship — $12.95
- ❑ #46: The Man Who Ruled in Hell — $13.95
- ❑ #47: Slaves of the Black Monarch — $13.95
- ❑ #48: Machineguns Over the White House — $13.95
- ❑ #49: The City That Dared Not Eat — $13.95
- ❑ #50: Master of the Flaming Horde — $13.95
- ❑ #51: Satan's Switchboard — $13.95
- ❑ #52: Legions of the Accursed Light — $13.95
- ❑ #53: The City of Lost Men — $13.95
- ❑ #54: The Grey Horde Creeps — $13.95
- ❑ #55: City of Whispering Death — $13.95
- ❑ #56: When Thousands Slept in Hell — $13.95
- ❑ #57: Satan's Shakles — $14.95
- ❑ #58: The Emperor From Hell — $14.95
- ❑ #59: The Devil's Candlesticks — $14.95
- ❑ #60: The City That Paid to Die — $14.95
- ❑ #61: The Spider at Bay — $14.95
- ❑ #62: Scourge of the Black Legions — $14.95
- ❑ #63: The Withering Death — $14.95
- ❑ #64: Claws of the Golden Dragon — $14.95
- ❑ #65: The Song of Death — $14.95
- ❑ #66: The Silver Death Reign — $14.95
- ❑ #67: Blight of the Blazing Eye — $14.95
- ❑ #68: King of the Fleshless Legion — $14.95
- ❑ #69: Rule of the Monster Men — $16.95
- ❑ #70: The Spider and the Slaves of Hell — $16.95
- ❑ #71: The Spider and the Fire God — $16.95
- ❑ #72: The Corpse Broker — $16.95
- ❑ #73: The Spider and the Eyeless Legion — $16.95
- ❑ #74: The Spider and the Faceless One — $16.95
- ❑ **_NEW:_** #75: Satan's Murder Machines — $16.95

THE WESTERN RAIDER

- ❑ #1: Guns of the Damned — $13.95
- ❑ #2: The Hawk Rides Back from Death — $13.95
- ❑ #3: Gun-Call for the Lost Legion — $13.95
- ❑ #4: The Law of Silver Trent — $13.95
- ❑ #5: The Gun-Prayer of Silver Trent — $13.95
- ❑ #6: Silver Trent Rides Alone — $13.95

CAPTAIN SATAN

- ❑ #1: The Mask of the Damned — $13.95
- ❑ #2: Parole for the Dead — $13.95
- ❑ #3: The Dead Man Express — $13.95
- ❑ #4: A Ghost Rides the Dawn — $13.95
- ❑ #5: The Ambassador From Hell — $13.95

DR. YEN SIN

- ❑ #1: Mystery of the Dragon's Shadow — $12.95
- ❑ #2: Mystery of the Golden Skull — $12.95
- ❑ #3: Mystery of the Singing Mummies — $12.95

THE MASKED MARKSMAN

- ❑ #1: Death Takes an Encore — $16.95
- ❑ **_NEW:_** #2: Death's Understudy — $16.95

ACE G-MAN

- ❑ #1: The Suicide Squad Reports for Death — $14.95
- ❑ #2: Coffins for the Suicide Squad — $14.95

❏ #3: Shells for the Suicide Squad	$14.95
❏ #4: The Suicide Squad in Corpse-Town	$14.95
❏ #5: Wanted–In Three Pine Coffins	$14.95
❏ #6: The Suicide Squad's Dawn Patrol	$14.95
❏ #7: Targets for the Flaming Arrow	$16.95

OPERATOR 5

❏ #1: The Masked Invasion	$13.95
❏ #2: The Invisible Empire	$13.95
❏ #3: The Yellow Scourge	$13.95
❏ #4: The Melting Death	$13.95
❏ #5: Cavern of the Damned	$13.95
❏ #6: Master of Broken Men	$13.95
❏ #7: Invasion of the Dark Legions	$13.95
❏ #8: The Green Death Mists	$13.95
❏ #9: Legions of Starvation	$13.95
❏ #10: The Red Invader	$13.95
❏ #11: The League of War-Monsters	$13.95
❏ #12: The Army of the Dead	$13.95
❏ #13: March of the Flame Marauders	$13.95
❏ #14: Blood Reign of the Dictator	$13.95
❏ #15: Invasion of the Yellow Warlords	$13.95
❏ #16: Legions of the Death Master	$13.95
❏ #17: Hosts of the Flaming Death	$13.95
❏ #18: Invasion of the Crimson Death Cult	$13.95
❏ #19: Attack of the Blizzard Men	$13.95
❏ #20: Scourge of the Invisible Death	$13.95
❏ #21: Raiders of the Red Death	$13.95
❏ #22: War-Dogs of the Green Destroyer	$13.95
❏ #23: Rockets From Hell	$13.95
❏ #24: War-Masters from the Orient	$13.95
❏ #25: Crime's Reign of Terror	$13.95
❏ #26: Death's Ragged Army	$13.95
❏ #27: Patriots' Death Battalion	$13.95
❏ #28: The Bloody Forty-five Days	$13.95
❏ #29: America's Plague Battalions	$13.95
❏ #30: Liberty's Suicide Legions	$13.95
❏ #31: Siege of the Thousand Patriots	$13.95
❏ #32: Patriots' Death March	$14.95
❏ #33: Revolt of the Lost Legions	$14.95
❏ #34: Drums of Destruction	$14.95
❏ #35: The Army Without a Country	$14.95
❏ #36: The Bloody Frontiers	$14.95
❏ #37: The Coming of the Mongol Hordes	$14.95
❏ #38: The Siege That Brought Black Death	$16.95
❏ #39: Revolt of the Devil Men	$16.95
❏ #40: The Suicide Battalion	$16.95
❏ #41: The Day of the Damned	$16.95

RED FINGER

❏ #1: Second-Hand Death	$24.95

G-8 AND HIS BATTLE ACES

❏ #1: The Bat Staffel	$13.95

CAPTAIN COMBAT

❏ #1: The Sky Beast of Berlin	$13.95
❏ #2: Red Wings For the Blood Battalion	$13.95
❏ #3: Low Ceiling For Nazi Hell Hawks	$13.95

DUSTY AYRES AND HIS BATTLE BIRDS

❏ #1: Black Lightning!	$13.95
❏ #2: Crimson Doom	$13.95
❏ #3: The Purple Tornado	$13.95
❏ #4: The Screaming Eye	$13.95
❏ #5: The Green Thunderbolt	$13.95
❏ #6: The Red Destroyer	$13.95
❏ #7: The White Death	$13.95
❏ #8: The Black Avenger	$13.95
❏ #9: The Silver Typhoon	$13.95
❏ #10: The Troposphere F-S	$13.95
❏ #11: The Blue Cyclone	$13.95
❏ #12: The Tesla Raiders	$13.95

MAVERICKS

❏ #1: Five Against the Law	$12.95
❏ #2: Mesquite Manhunters	$12.95
❏ #3: Bait for the Lobo Pack	$12.95
❏ #4: Doc Grimson's Outlaw Posse	$12.95
❏ #5: Charlie Parr's Gunsmoke Cure	$12.95

THE MYSTERIOUS WU FANG

❏ #1: The Case of the Six Coffins	$12.95
❏ #2: The Case of the Scarlet Feather	$12.95
❏ #3: The Case of the Yellow Mask	$12.95
❏ #4: The Case of the Suicide Tomb	$12.95
❏ #5: The Case of the Green Death	$12.95
❏ #6: The Case of the Black Lotus	$12.95
❏ #7: The Case of the Hidden Scourge	$12.95

THE SECRET 6

❏ #1: The Red Shadow	$13.95
❏ #2: House of Walking Corpses	$13.95
❏ #3: The Monster Murders	$13.95
❏ #4: The Golden Alligator	$13.95

CAPTAIN ZERO

❏ #1: City of Deadly Sleep	$13.95
❏ #2: The Mark of Zero!	$13.95
❏ #3: The Golden Murder Syndicate	$13.95